## Liz w

Chance might have been a bit rough around the edges socially, but his kiss was decidedly skilled, evoking feelings Liz hadn't experienced in years. She resisted only a moment before responding, her lips softening, parting beneath his.

There had been something about this man that had drawn her from the moment she'd seen him standing in her office. Something in his eyes, something in his smile that melted her defenses—even after he had announced his intention to prevent his brother from marrying her niece.

Now his kiss spoke to her of pleasures only imagined before, of a passion that went beyond anything she'd ever known with any other man.

It was a long time before Liz could make herself pull away. Still close enough that she could feel his breath on her cheek, she looked into his eyes. "I can't do this, Chance...."

"*This* has nothing to do with Phillip and Sara. It has everything to do with us," Chance insisted.

Fascinated by the number of people involved in the production of weddings, from consultants and dress designers to florists and photographers, **Gina Wilkins** thought it would be perfect to explore how three women—friends and business associates—all find the men of their dreams when they work together on a wedding. In Temptation's three-book miniseries VEILS & VOWS, Gina introduces us to Liz Archer and her best friends, Devon and Holly. To discover how Devon and Holly get their men, look for *Designs on Love* (June) and *At Long Last Love* (August).

## Books by Gina Wilkins

**HARLEQUIN TEMPTATION**
283—COULD IT BE MAGIC
299—CHANGING THE RULES
309—AFTER HOURS
337—A REBEL AT HEART
353—A PERFECT STRANGER
369—HOTLINE

Don't miss any of our special offers. Write to us at the following address for information on our newest releases.

Harlequin Reader Service
P.O. Box 1397, Buffalo, NY 14240
Canadian address: P.O. Box 603,
Fort Erie, Ont. L2A 5X3

# Taking a Chance on Love

## GINA WILKINS

## *Harlequin Books*

TORONTO • NEW YORK • LONDON
AMSTERDAM • PARIS • SYDNEY • HAMBURG
STOCKHOLM • ATHENS • TOKYO • MILAN
MADRID • WARSAW • BUDAPEST • AUCKLAND

For Ken Payne, a good friend who reads my books and who was the inspiration for a recent hero. Thanks.

Published April 1992

ISBN 0-373-25492-X

TAKING A CHANCE ON LOVE

# Prologue

FOR THE THIRD TIME, Chance Cassidy angrily scanned the letter in his hand. Disgusted, he crumpled it into a ball. "The coward," he muttered. "He could have at least had the guts to tell me to my face."

Huddled in her wheelchair, his stepmother, Nadine, wiped at her tears with an unsteady hand. "We don't even know this girl. How could he marry someone he hasn't even introduced to his family? No wonder he won't come home for Thanksgiving. He'll spend it with *her* and her father, making their plans behind our backs."

"They're not married yet, Mother. He said they're planning the wedding for the end of June. That gives us seven months."

Nadine sniffed and looked doubtful. "You know how Phillip is when he makes up his mind about something. He'll never listen to us."

"He'll listen to me," Chance countered flatly, "if I have to tie him to a chair to get his full attention."

Nadine bit her lower lip. "Now, Chance, don't lose your temper. I'm sure Phillip thinks he's in love with the girl. You'll only make him more determined to go through with this if you charge off to Atlanta and forbid him to have anything more to do with her."

"Give me credit for a little more sense than that. But I do plan to leave for Atlanta as soon as I can get away. I want to meet the girl and check into this company her father owns. Phillip seems to think the guy's offering him a helluva future—a lot more than I can offer, apparently."

Nadine winced at his tone. Guiltily Chance realized that he hadn't concealed his hurt. He shoved his hands, crumpled letter and all, into the pockets of his dusty jeans.

"I've got to get cleaned up," he mumbled, looking away from Nadine's pale, unhappy face. "Don't worry about this. I'll take care of it." Ever since his father had died when he was fifteen and Phillip was five, he'd always taken care of things. He had no intention of allowing his younger brother to rush impulsively into marriage without guidance.

He headed for his bedroom, stripped off his dirty, sweat-stained shirt the moment he stepped through the door. *First a shower*, he decided, *and then a few telephone calls*. He wanted to find out all he could about Neal Archer and his daughter, Sara, before leaving for Atlanta. He intended to be well prepared when he confronted Phillip.

His gaze fell on the little carved wooden box sitting on his dresser. If Phillip thought he was going to get the ring for this girl he'd suddenly decided to marry, he could just think again. That ring had been entrusted to Chance, and he'd always hoped it would be his own wife who'd wear it. Unfortunately, at thirty-four, he hadn't yet found a woman he considered worthy of that particular honor, or with whom he wanted to spend the rest of his life. He knew some might consider him arrogant and overly discriminating; but how could Phillip, ten years younger than himself, be certain *he* had found the right woman for marriage?

"We'll just have to see about that, Phillip," Chance muttered, reaching for the snap of his jeans, his fierce gaze still locked on the wooden box. "I'm going to find out exactly what Sara Archer and her father are after."

# 1

"AND WHEN THE OFFICIANT pronounces them married, the couple wants to strip to the buff in front of the audience to symbolize that they are beginning life anew, dressed the same way they began life the first time." Liz Archer's voice shook with a combination of amusement and aversion as she told her two best friends of the strangest request she'd ever received as a wedding consultant.

Devon Fleming shuddered with distaste. "Thank goodness they didn't approach me about designing the wedding dress. I don't think I could bring myself to create a Velcro-fastened, strip-away gown."

Toying with the camera that was her constant companion, Holly Baldwin giggled. "It might have been a fun ceremony to shoot," she said with a touch of regret. "Of course, I probably would've been arrested, but it would make a nice change from the smile-and-freeze shots I usually take at weddings."

Liz grimaced and shook her head, causing a strand of blond hair to fall into her eyes. She shoved it back. "You didn't meet this couple. Believe me, these are not people you want to see nude, much less immortalized on film."

"Dogs, huh?"

"Woof, woof." Sighing, Liz looked at the stack of papers and planners on her desk. "And I thought I'd heard them all."

"You've only been in this business five years or so," Devon pointed out dryly. "I predict you'll get weirder requests than that. There's no limit to the imagination of people under the influence of passionate love, it seems. Remember the woman last year who wanted me to design a wedding gown modeled after a harem outfit to show that she was a slave to love?"

Now Liz shuddered. "I remember," she said grimly. "By the time the wedding was over, I was ready to strangle the jerk she married. He hardly let her breathe without his permission. She may have liked it then, but I'll bet the novelty has worn off by now." Her friends nodded, recalling Liz's stories about her domineering ex-husband.

Liz had married young and impetuously. Almost immediately following the wedding, her husband had begun jealously guarding her every movement, attempting to isolate her from friends and family—even monitoring her telephone calls and mail. It had taken her two years to realize that nothing she could do would change him, nor make that ill-fated marriage work.

"Well, *I'm* going to have the most traditional wedding you could possibly plan, Liz," Holly announced airily, after noting Liz's dark mood at the memory of her disastrous marriage. "I want it all—a gaggle of bridesmaids in pastel organdy, enough candles to risk a major fire, a wedding cake big enough to feed a small country, the scent of orange blossoms polluting the air."

"A *gaggle* of bridesmaids?" Devon chaffed.

"Whatever they're called," Holly replied with a wave of her hand. "And I want you to design the dress, Devon. Yards and yards of white lace with a train that goes all the way to the next county, and a tiny waist and lots of bosom showing to offset the virginal effect."

"Holly, love, you couldn't show lots of bosom if I cut the gown to your waist," Devon said teasingly, eyeing Holly's slim figure concealed beneath a colorful over-size sweater.

"And aren't you forgetting something in all this wedding planning?" Liz pointed out. "Like the fact that you aren't even dating anyone at the moment? Don't you think maybe there should be a groom involved?"

"Oh, you two are so depressingly prosaic," Holly complained, looking from Liz to Devon in obviously exaggerated exasperation. "I'm still searching for a groom and I fully intend to find one. As for the other problem—" scowling, she looked down at her practically nonexistent bosom "—maybe I should order one of those Bust-O-Matics out of the back of the latest 'confessions' magazine."

Liz couldn't help laughing. She could always depend on Holly to make her laugh, no matter what kind of day she'd had.

"Liz, looks like the family is here." Holly drew Liz's attention to the two men and a glowingly pretty young brunette who stood in the open doorway that led into the now empty outer office where a receptionist usually greeted callers.

"Hi, Sara. How's it going, Phillip?" Holly said warmly.

Liz hadn't expected anyone to drop in after five on a Tuesday afternoon, but she wasn't at all displeased to see her brother, Neal, his daughter, Sara, and Sara's boyfriend, Phillip Cassidy. She smiled in greeting. "Well, hello. How was the business trip to Denver, Neal?"

He shrugged expressively. "Just the usual business trip. But we're interrupting you. We'll wait out here until you're finished."

"Don't be silly, it's only a gossip session," Holly quickly explained, jumping down from her perch on one corner of the cherry conference table. "Devon and I stopped by to chat with Liz on our way to an early movie. We were just leaving."

Devon picked up her purse and stood, preparing to leave.

Liz detained them with an upheld hand. "Before you go, I'd like you to finally meet my brother. This is Sara's father, Neal Archer."

Since Sara often worked for Liz during school breaks, Liz had introduced her to her friends years earlier. Subsequently, Sara often joined the threesome on out-

ings to dinners and movies, eventually becoming re-
garded as an honorary niece by Holly and Devon.
Through Sara, Phillip had met Liz's friends. Neal,
however, had never met them, as he was generally too
involved with his business to socialize. His rare free
time was dedicated strictly to family.

Turning to Neal, Liz motioned toward her friends.
"I know you've heard me talk about Devon Fleming and
Holly Baldwin. Devon designs and makes breathtak-
ing wedding gowns, and Holly's the best wedding and
portrait photographer I've ever known."

Typically, Devon flushed lightly at the compliment.
Holly only grinned more brightly, accepting the praise
as her due.

Sara looked avidly from Liz to her friends, her hand
gripped tightly in Phillip's. "I'm so glad you're all here,"
she said, her dark eyes sparkling. "I have an announcement to make and I want you all to hear. Actually, I
want to hire all of you. You, too, Aunt Liz."

Liz looked from her blissful twenty-year-old niece to
the proudly smiling young man at her side. "Sara! You
mean . . . ?"

"Phillip and I are getting married," Sara confirmed,
with a dreamy smile. "In late June. Isn't it wonderful?"

Liz turned to her brother, studying his rather rueful
smile. Their little girl, getting married? Sara would turn
twenty-one in May, just before graduating from college. She was too young to get married! Too inexperi-
enced to take such a life-altering step! She'd only been

dating Phillip for a few months. How could Neal look so calm about this?

And then she realized that Sara was waiting for a response. And Liz knew exactly what response she'd give. Though her first reaction had been denial, she'd been expecting this news from the first time Sara had introduced her to Phillip. Liz worked with people in love every day. Phillip and Sara were deeply in love, which was vividly apparent to anyone who spent more than a few minutes in their company. "Why, yes, Sara. That's wonderful news," she said.

Neal's smile deepened, his dark eyes mocking her. He obviously knew Liz was shaken by the announcement, though she'd tried to disguise her reaction. It had always annoyed her that Neal could read her so easily when she'd never been able to do likewise with him. She couldn't begin to guess at his true feelings about his daughter's engagement. "When did this happen, Sara?" Liz asked, ignoring her brother for the moment.

"Phillip proposed Friday night. I think he surprised himself as much as he did me," Sara added. "But I'm not letting him change his mind."

"No need to worry about that," Phillip responded with a wide grin.

"You've been engaged for three and a half days and just got around to telling your only aunt?" Liz demanded with mock sternness.

Sara giggled at her tone, but explained earnestly, "Sorry, Aunt Liz, but of course, I had to tell Daddy first.

So I couldn't say anything about it until he got back from Denver. But we came straight here afterward, didn't we, Daddy?"

"Immediately," Neal gravely confirmed.

"Please say you'll do my gown," Sara asked eagerly, turning to Devon. "The gowns you design are so gorgeous. I've always wanted you to do mine when the time came."

"Of course, I will," Devon assured her, smiling as she appraised Sara's proportions with experienced brown eyes. "It shouldn't be hard to design a gown that will please you. With your figure, you can wear almost any style you like."

Sara blushed at the compliment, casting a glance toward Phillip. Liz observed that Phillip was busily admiring his fiancée's shape in response to Devon's comment. She swallowed hard at the realization that the baby girl she'd once bathed and diapered would be this man's wife in just seven months.

She glanced again at Neal, who seemed to be assessing Devon and Holly. Since they were both standing behind her, Liz couldn't tell which of the two had captured her brother's attention. Probably it was Devon. She'd always thought that Devon and Neal might make a nice couple. Neal, who had just turned forty, was a very successful businessman and a very eligible bachelor. He was serious and thoroughly unpretentious, which made him a good match for Devon, who was a bit shy and preferred a quiet life-style herself. Had Liz been inclined to play matchmaker—which she was not—she might have introduced them previously.

Then Holly broke the silence in the room. "You'll be a beautiful bride, Sara, especially in one of Devon's creations. And I'd be happy to talk to you about your wedding photographs. I always love taking pictures of beautiful brides and handsome grooms." She winked saucily at Phillip.

Still talking, she carefully stored her camera in its bag, gathered her other things and headed toward the door, with Devon close behind. "We have to leave now or we're going to be late for the movie, right, Dev? Besides, I know y'all want to talk family stuff in the wake of this grand announcement."

She paused in front of Neal, peering up at him from beneath her copper bangs. "It was especially nice to meet you, Mr. Archer. Liz has told us a lot about you. She's even said some pretty nice things—for a sister."

Neal chuckled. Surreptitiously studying him, Liz felt that he was regarding Holly as indulgently as he did Sara's college friends.

"Please call me Neal," he suggested. "And it was very nice to meet you, too, Holly. We'll see each other again."

"You bet." Holly gave him a bright smile, then waved to Liz. "See you later, Liz." She exuberantly hugged Sara and Phillip before leaving, followed by Devon, whose farewells were typically more reserved.

Neal cleared his throat. "Holly's quite a talker, isn't she? No wonder Sara's always liked her so much."

"Yes, she's very hyper. But at least you never have to worry about being bored when Holly's around." Liz said.

Neal grinned. "That I believe."

"They're both extremely attractive, aren't they, Daddy? And they're both single, aren't they, Aunt Liz?" Sara eyed her father speculatively.

"Both single," Liz confirmed, smiling at the look her brother leveled at his daughter.

"No matchmaking, Sara, remember?" he growled. "You know what I told you."

To Liz he added, "She has this idea that I'll be lonely after she and Phillip are married. She's decided to try to marry me off, as well." He grimaced.

"Hardier souls than you have tried and failed," Liz teasingly warned her niece.

Sara shrugged good-naturedly. "Well, gee, it doesn't hurt to try. I think Daddy needs to be married, don't you? Our house is too big for just one person."

"Are you kidding? I'm looking forward to it. It'll be the first time in my life I've lived on my own," Neal admitted. "I may just delegate some of the business to Phillip and take off for the Bahamas to kick back and vegetate for a while."

"Oh, sure you will," Sara jeered, affectionately punching his arm. "Ol' Workaholic Archer on vacation? This I'd love to see."

"I've taken you on vacations," he protested.

"Sure. You also carried a cellular phone through Disney World," she reminded him with a dramatic sigh.

"Not quite," he responded with a laugh.

"Close enough."

*Neal definitely needs rescuing,* Liz decided, and began questioning Sara about her wedding plans.

"You *will* organize my wedding for me, won't you, Aunt Liz?" Sara asked anxiously. "I know I've helped you do dozens of them, but I want to make sure mine is planned perfectly."

"Of course, I will, Sara. But you didn't want to start today, did you? It would be better if we set up an appointment so I can have a planning package worked up for you, as I do with my other clients."

Sara giggled. "I think I can wait that long. But I really wish you could go with us to Englewood tomorrow for the holiday, Aunt Liz. We'll miss you."

"It's hard to believe someone's really getting married on Thanksgiving," Phillip commented.

Liz nodded. "The groom's a serviceman. It was the only night he had clear before being reassigned to a new base. They're having a full military wedding. It should be beautiful."

"Can't you join us later in the week? Friday, maybe, after the wedding's over?" Sara pleaded.

"Yeah, Liz, how about it?" Neal echoed. "It'll give us all a chance to get away for a few days and spend the time as a family."

Regretfully, Liz shook her head. "I would love to, but I can't. I have another wedding on Saturday, and several appointments scheduled for Monday. It's going to be a very busy week for me."

"You'll be alone for the entire holiday weekend," Sara said, obviously concerned. "Maybe we should stay here. We could have a late Thanksgiving at our house Friday evening, instead. This trip to the vacation condo in Florida was a spur-of-the-moment idea, anyway."

Liz could tell that her brother and Phillip were both ready to agree without hesitation. Touched by their generosity, she said adamantly, "You will not give up your plans for me. Honestly, Sara, I'll be so busy we'd hardly have time to see each other, anyway. You know how hectic wedding weeks are for me. Especially with two weddings two days apart."

"If you're sure . . ." Sara capitulated.

"I'm sure. Next week you and Phillip and I will sit down and start planning the most beautiful wedding Atlanta has ever seen, okay?"

Sara beamed. "Oh, yes."

"Why don't you two run on to your party now," Neal suggested. "I'll stay and help Liz lock up her office."

Sara glanced at the Rolex watch Neal had given her for her twentieth birthday. "Goodness, we *had* better hurry or we'll be late." She stepped into her aunt's arms.

Liz hugged Sara tightly, clinging a bit longer than usual. Sara had grown up so quickly, she thought sadly.

Since she had no children of her own, she had always enjoyed her close relationship with Sara.

Only after Sara and Phillip had left did Liz allow herself to wipe her tears away. "Oh, Neal," she whispered, "she's so young."

"Sara's almost a year older than I was when she was born," he reminded her gently. "And she's always known exactly what she wanted, even when she was little."

Liz smiled shakily. "I know." She dried her cheeks with a tissue. "So you really don't mind that she's getting married?"

Neal sighed. "I've been expecting it since she brought Phillip home for the first time, three months ago. There was just something about the way she looked at him...."

He shrugged somewhat sheepishly. "All right, I'll admit I resisted the idea at first. Like you, I was worried that she's too young. But she's got her mind set on this. Phillip seems like a mature young man. He'll be a fine son-in-law and a good employee. She could have done much worse," Neal said reassuringly.

"What about his family?" Liz asked, curious. "He doesn't talk about them much. His mother and brother live in Alabama, don't they?"

"Birmingham," Neal confirmed.

"I wonder how they feel about his engagement. He *has* told them?"

"He said he sent them a letter Saturday," Neal replied, frowning. "They'd have gotten it today, most likely. I assume they aren't very close or he'd have told them in person. I'll try to find out more about them while we're vacationing together this week."

So that was the reason why Neal had suggested spending a few days at his vacation place in Florida. He would use the time to find out all there was left to know about his prospective son-in-law. She should have known Neal wouldn't take his daughter's engagement lightly—despite his relaxed attitude.

She reached for some of the files scattered on her desk, gathering them into an orderly pile. She hated leaving a mess behind when she left her office in the evening. Neal watched her with amusement. "One of the folders is a quarter inch out of line from the others," he teased.

"Kiss it, Neal."

He laughed at her familiar response. She glanced up, pleased to see that his laughter had eased the tension in his handsome face, making him appear much younger. Sara was right—Neal should find someone to share his life with. He'd be very lonely after his daughter moved out.

Loneliness was something Liz was all too familiar with; something she didn't want her brother to have to experience. Maybe she should reconsider her personal taboo against matchmaking. And maybe *she* should make another foray into the dating scene.

But what was she thinking? She was certainly in no hurry to remarry. All this talk of weddings must be getting to her. Rather ironic for someone who organized weddings for a living, she reflected ruefully, glancing at the gold lettering on her outer-office door as she locked it: Special Events, Inc. She'd worked long and hard to establish her business and make it a success. She loved her work, found it very fulfilling. There was nothing missing in her life. Absolutely nothing at all. She was perfectly content with things the way they were.

She turned to Neal. "Got plans for the evening?" she asked.

"No, for once I'm appointment-free."

"Then, how about treating your sister to dinner?"

He held out his hand. "I can't think of anything I'd rather do," he assured her.

LATE THE NEXT AFTERNOON, Chance Cassidy hesitated in front of the glass door. Special Events. What a stupid name for a business. No comparison to his company's name. Cassidy Construction Company. Simple, straightforward, self-explanatory. He shoved the door open.

The lobby made him feel even more irritated and disoriented. Everything in the room seemed to be pink. Huge portraits of misty-eyed, lace-gowned brides hung on the walls and there were enough flowers in the room to fill a greenhouse. With each step he took toward the reception desk his boots left deep imprints in the plush carpet. No wonder his brother had been brainwashed into agreeing to have an overblown wedding.

A slightly overweight brunette looked up from her computer, her fingers pausing on the keyboard. "May I help you?" she asked.

Chance was quite certain he wasn't the usual type of customer. After all, he hardly looked like a blushing groom, he thought grimly, shoving his hands into the pockets of his jacket. "I'm looking for Elizabeth Archer. Is that you?"

The woman lifted one dark eyebrow. "Ms. Archer is my employer. She's in a meeting with clients at the moment. May I help you?"

"No." He didn't move.

The woman cleared her throat. "Then perhaps you'd like to have a seat until Ms. Archer is available? She should be able to see you in another fifteen minutes or so. This is her final appointment for the day. We usually close at five," she added, looking up at the white wicker clock on the wall above her desk to emphasize that it was getting very close to that time.

He exhaled impatiently. "I'll wait." Sighting a row of cushioned rose chintz chairs against the wall, he scowled and selected the nearest one. A selection of magazines lay scattered on a small table at his elbow. He thumbed through a few unenthusiastically. *Bride's, Modern Bride, Bridal Guide*. Great! More brides!

Grunting his disgust, he crossed his arms over his chest and stared down at his boots.

*What a stupid way for someone to make a living! Can't people plan their own weddings, for Pete's sake?* How much trouble could it involve, anyway? Choose a date, find a minister or a JP, buy a fancy dress off a rack and show up on time for the ceremony. It wasn't like putting up a fifty-story building. Now *that* took planning and organization.

Twenty long, boring minutes had passed when finally the door to Elizabeth Archer's office opened. Chance looked up in relief, ready to meet Neal Archer's sister—the only person able to put him in contact with Phillip at the moment.

A young woman, obviously a prospective bride, came through the door. She snuggled close to the side of the prospective groom, a heavyset young man, grinning so fatuously that Chance wanted to spit. Was this the way Phillip looked around his Sara?

Then he noticed the woman who followed the couple into the reception area. "Give me a call first thing Monday and let me know what menu you've chosen for your reception," she said. "I'll need to notify the caterer as quickly as possible."

"I will, Liz," the young woman promised. "You think I should go with the raspberry trifle?"

"It's a fabulous dessert. And the colors go nicely with your theme. Think about it."

Chance never saw the couple leave. Instead, he concentrated on the woman who stood outside the doorway of her office, watching him with curious, dark blue eyes.

She was beautiful. One of the most beautiful women he'd ever seen. She had the type of skin he'd heard compared to porcelain—pale, smooth, unblemished. Her blue eyes were thickly lashed, her high cheekbones the palest pink, her mouth lush. Her hair was blond, shoulder-length, brushed casually back from her face. She was on the tall side—maybe five-seven, five-eight—slender, but curved in all the right places. Though she could have been twenty, for all he knew, something about her made him place her closer to his own age. Maybe it was the glint of experience in her expression when she studied him as frankly as he studied her.

Classy, he thought, eyeing her white linen suit. Probably snooty. Definitely out of his league.

"May I help you?" Her voice was as cultured and well-bred as her appearance.

He had to remind himself again that she was Neal Archer's sister to resurrect the anger he'd felt twenty minutes earlier. Rising from the chair, he took advantage of his height to loom over her, his eyes narrowing as they locked with hers. "My name is Chance Cassidy. I'm Phillip Cassidy's brother. I want you to tell me how to get in touch with him. Then I want to know what the hell is going on."

Elizabeth Archer lifted one delicate eyebrow in reaction to his curtness. "You may as well go on home, Marcy," she told her receptionist, who gaped at them openmouthed. "Just switch the phones over to the service."

"I really don't mind waiting, Liz."

"That's not necessary. I have a few more things to do before I lock up. Have a nice Thanksgiving weekend, Marcy. I'll see you Monday morning."

"All right. Hope everything goes smoothly with the wedding tomorrow. And that you manage to find a little time to enjoy Thanksgiving."

Liz smiled at her. This was a mouth shaped for passion, he found himself thinking, and brought himself up short. He really couldn't imagine this cool, poised woman looking hot and rumpled from uninhibited lovemaking. And he had no use for women who believed themselves to be too good for honest sweat.

She waved one hand toward the open door to her office. "Please come in, Mr. Cassidy."

Eyeing her suspiciously, Chance nodded and motioned for her to precede him. Without hesitation, she walked through, leaving him to stare after her, his gaze lingering on the sway of her slim hips beneath her linen skirt. He cleared his throat, reminding himself that he was only there to find out about Phillip's hasty engagement—and, if possible, to put an end to it.

Something told him that Elizabeth Archer wasn't going to want anything to do with him once he'd outlined his mission.

# 2

LIZ GATHERED her scattered notes for the wedding of the couple who had just left her office, arranging them in a stack. Those mechanical motions gave her an opportunity to regain her composure, which seemed to have been lost sometime during the initial exchange of glances with the man.

She couldn't define her reactions to him. His tanned face was too hard, too bluntly carved to be described as handsome. His hair was tobacco brown, carelessly brushed back from his forehead. His eyes were hazel, framed by squint lines at the corners. He was muscular—the result, she suspected, of hard manual labor.

*Uncompromisingly male, in the most old-fashioned sense of the word,* she decided as she faced him with a polite, professional smile. "Now, why don't we begin again, Mr. Cassidy. How may I help you?"

It was immediately apparent that he didn't care for the unintentionally patronizing tone she'd used in hopes of soothing him. "You can tell me where my brother is," he said, scowling.

"Phillip is with my brother and my niece at their vacation condo in Florida," Liz explained calmly, crossing her arms at her waist as she leaned back against a corner of the conference table. "They left this afternoon to spend the next five days there. They plan to return late Monday afternoon, so they'll avoid the holiday travel crowds on Sunday. There's no secrecy involved. All you had to do was ask."

"I *did* ask," Chance growled. "I asked his roommate, who could only tell me that Phillip was somewhere out of the state. I asked how I could get in touch with him and the guy had no idea. I called your brother's office and was told that Neal Archer was out until next week and that they could not divulge personal information about their employer to callers. I asked your brother's next-door neighbor, who could only give me your name and the address of this business. Is it any wonder that I'm running out of patience?"

No. Chance Cassidy didn't appear to be a particularly patient man. Just the opposite, in fact. "I'm sorry you've been so inconvenienced. I have the number of the condo. If you need to reach Phillip immediately, you're welcome to use the telephone on my desk."

"I really didn't want to discuss my business with him over the phone," he muttered. "I'd have called before coming here if that was all I wanted."

"Then perhaps you'd like the address so you can join him there," she suggested. She couldn't help wondering if Chance had arrived in response to Phillip's letter announcing his engagement to Sara. If so, it was clear he wasn't pleased with the news. She bristled at the thought that this unfriendly man could threaten Sara's happiness.

"No, I don't want to join them at the *vacation condo*," he said, stressing the last two words just enough to make them sound almost like an oath. "I have a business to run in Birmingham. I was hoping to be back there tomorrow."

She tried not to let it show that his attitude was irritating her, but she suspected her voice reflected her impatience when she spoke. "Then I'm afraid you're out of luck, Mr. Cassidy. You really should have called before leaving home."

His jaw clenched and she could tell he was biting back a sarcastic remark. He scanned her office, pausing when he spotted the framed needlepoint sampler hanging above her desk. Devon had given it to Liz several years before, and she couldn't imagine why Chance seemed so annoyed by the quotation, "Make no little plans; they have no magic to stir men's blood."

"I haven't eaten since breakfast and I'm not at my best when I'm hungry," he said with a candid abruptness that amused her. "I'd like to talk to you over dinner."

"Talk about what?" she asked, startled by the invitation—or had it been an invitation? It had sounded almost like a command.

"My kid brother sent me a letter telling me he's marrying a girl he's never even mentioned before," Chance replied evenly. "Our long-standing plan for us to go into business together has been scrubbed since he's accepting a job with his future father-in-law. I didn't even get a phone call—just that damned letter. Now do you find it strange that I'd like to know a *little* more about what's going on here?"

Put that way, it didn't sound strange at all. Catching a glimpse of hurt in his dark eyes, she imagined how she and Neal would have felt if they had learned about Sara's engagement from a letter. Yet she remained oddly ambivalent about having dinner with Chance. Nevertheless she owed it to Sara to at least attempt to smooth the way before the inevitable confrontation between Phillip and his older brother.

"Look, I know it's short notice. You probably have other plans. I just thought—"

"All right, Mr. Cassidy. I'll have dinner with you." She managed a weak smile. "After all, we're almost family."

The momentary lightening of his expression that had accompanied her acceptance vanished. "Not quite," he said grimly, confirming her suspicion that he intended to do what he could to end his brother's engagement.

*How incredibly arrogant!* She snatched her purse. "I'll make you something to eat at my place," she offered impulsively. "I'm sure neither of us wants to hold a personal discussion in a restaurant."

"Fine." He hesitated, then added belatedly, "Uh—thanks."

"Do you have a car, Mr. Cassidy, or did you take a cab from the airport?"

"Call me Chance. And I drove from Birmingham."

"Then you can follow me. Just let me turn out the lights and lock up."

"Fine."

"Fine." Her eyes met his and held for one brief, taut moment in which she issued a clear challenge. She would not allow him to interfere with Sara's happiness.

She was wholly unprepared for his smile, accepting her challenge. It was dangerous and unmistakably sexy.

Clearing her throat, she turned quickly away. As she reached for the light switch, it occurred to her that Sara and Phillip weren't the only ones who should beware of Chance Cassidy.

KEEPING HIS DUSTY pickup close behind her red sports car on the drive to Liz's home, Chance vowed to be on his best behavior there and to find out all he could about the Archer family before deciding what to do next. He'd seen the suspicion, the wariness in Liz Archer's eyes when she'd invited him to dinner. It wouldn't serve his purpose to alienate her just yet. It also wouldn't hurt to have someone in the Archer family on his side when the inevitable confrontation took place, though Chance wasn't sure about obtaining Liz's support.

After having seen Neal Archer's huge Tudor-style mansion, Chance wasn't particularly surprised that Liz lived in an expensive-looking, "security" apartment

building in what seemed to be a trendy, upwardly mo-
bile neighborhood. It fit her, somehow. He followed her
past the guard stationed in the lobby to a bank of ele-
vators. Again he wondered if Elizabeth Archer ever just
let her hair down enough to enjoy herself. Had she ever
been hiking, camping, fishing? Ever ridden a motor-
cycle, climbed a mountain, swigged a cold beer after a
rowdy, sweaty game of touch football? Or was her idea
of a rousing good time an evening at the ballet or an
afternoon in a museum?

He imagined her in something long and sleek and
sophisticated. Black, probably. Strapless. With maybe
a glitter of diamonds at her slender throat, and her
blond hair swept into a neat twist that dared a man to
take it down. He was utterly astonished to feel his body
reacting with unexpected force to that image. What was
happening? He'd never been interested in this kind of
woman before. And even if Elizabeth Archer was his
type, he had a snowball's chance in hell with her once
she figured out that he was determined to end her niece's
engagement.

The elevator stopped at the tenth floor. Neither
Chance nor Liz had spoken during the ride up. He
trailed her to a door halfway down the hall on the right
and waited patiently while she unlocked it. She twisted
the knob and glanced up at him, her wariness still
clearly evident in her dark blue eyes. "Welcome to my
home, Mr. Cassidy," she said with a hint of mockery.

He nodded and walked into her apartment.

He'd expected frills and pastels like what he'd seen in her office. Some Victorian antiques, ruffly throw pillows, dainty porcelain knickknacks. Instead, her furnishings were distinctly modern, the colors bold. Dominating the living room was an oversize couch upholstered in a floral print in deep greens, bright blues and Chinese red. Solid-color cushions were piled at the ends—and not one of them was ruffled. Low tables finished in glossy black lacquer held unusual objets d'art; there were bright, modern paintings on the walls. For some reason, Chance had the feeling that every item in the room had been carefully selected—and by Liz, not some interior decorator.

He caught her observing him with an enigmatic smile. "Surprised?" she asked. "I bet you were expecting flowered chintzes and lace."

"How'd you know?" he asked with a sheepish grin.

She shrugged. "You wouldn't be the first."

Chance slipped out of his leather jacket. "It's a nice place."

She reached for the jacket. "Thank you. I'll put that in the bedroom for you. Make yourself comfortable. I'll be right back."

Was her bedroom as modern as her living room? Why was the thought of her bedroom making his body stir again like a teenager's? Dammit, what was the matter with him? It wasn't as if he'd never been alone with a beautiful woman before—though he'd met few women he considered as beautiful as this one. What

was it about Elizabeth Archer that made him react so
strongly?

Grimly he reminded himself of his reason for being
here in the first place. He intended to use this time with
her to find out everything he could about the Archer
family—and, if he was lucky, to convince Liz that
Phillip and Sara were too young to be married and
needed the guidance of their older, supposedly wiser
relatives. That was all.

He roamed the room, ending up at a tall black-
lacquer bookcase. Startled, he saw several of his favorite books on her shelves. It annoyed him a bit,
though he couldn't exactly say why. He'd felt the same
way when he'd seen that sampler on the wall of her office. The quotation from Daniel Hudson Burnham, an
architect whose work he'd always admired, hung in his
own office, though not in fancy needlepoint. It was
disconcerting that this woman with whom he seemed
to have so little in common shared a few of his tastes.

Liz rejoined him, and he noted that she'd changed out
of her suit into a simple white blouse and pleated teal
slacks. "Could I get you a drink before I start dinner?"
she asked in her attractively husky voice. "I have tea,
beer or wine—or there's something stronger in the li-
quor cabinet, if you'd prefer."

"You have beer?"

She smiled. "My brother likes it. Is that what you
want?"

"Yes, thanks."

"I'll get it. There's a television in the cabinet in the corner if you'd like to watch the news while I cook dinner. It should be ready in about a half hour."

*The gracious hostess.* And yet he still sensed that she wasn't completely comfortable with him. He had the feeling that men like him didn't often invade her sanctuary, and was rather pleased at the thought.

FORTY-FIVE MINUTES later, Chance came to the conclusion that either Elizabeth Archer didn't often cook for men or the men she knew didn't do enough honest labor to work up real appetites. The meal she served consisted of a small salad, a few ounces of grilled fish in a creamy sauce and a modest portion of steamed vegetables. It tasted good, but Chance hadn't eaten all day. He repressed a sigh. As soon as he left, he'd go for a hamburger.

They talked politely enough during the meal. Liz asked about his family. Chance explained that Phillip was his half brother, Chance's mother having died when he was seven. Their father had married Nadine a year later, and Phillip was born soon after Chance's tenth birthday.

"Your stepmother lives with you in Birmingham?" Liz asked, cutting into her fish.

Chance nodded, carefully chewing a broccoli floret. He hoped that eating slowly would make the undersize portions of food more satisfying. He swallowed and reached for his glass of ice tea. "My stepmother is confined to a wheelchair," he explained. "She has multiple sclerosis. She gets along pretty well, on the whole, but I like having her close where I can keep an eye on her."

"That's very considerate of you," Liz said, studying him thoughtfully from across the small table.

Chance shrugged and avoided her gaze by looking down at his nearly empty plate. "She's been my mother for twenty-seven years. I take care of my family."

"That's why you're here, isn't it?" she asked. "You think you have a responsibility to make certain Phillip isn't making a serious mistake by marrying my niece."

He lifted his eyes slowly to hers. "Yes," he answered.

"Phillip is an adult," she pointed out. "He's twenty-four."

"He's my kid brother," Chance corrected flatly. "I'm not going to stand back and let him ruin his life."

"Chance—"

Before she could continue, he changed the subject. "Tell me about your business," he suggested. "How long have you been in the wedding game?"

"I've been in this *game*," she replied, stressing the word to express her displeasure with it, "for nearly five years. Ironically enough, I went to work as a wedding consultant only a couple of years after my own divorce."

He looked over automatically at her bare left hand. The idea of another man's ring irked him. "How long were you married?"

"Two years. Have you ever been married?" It occurred to Liz that she knew almost nothing about the man sitting across her table from her. She assumed he wasn't married now; was there a woman who held an important place in his life? But why did that matter to her?

"No. I haven't had time," Chance admitted. "I've been too busy running my own company."

"You're in construction?" Liz had heard Phillip mention his brother's firm—Cassidy Construction Company.

Chance nodded and speared his fork into the last bit of carrot on his plate. Watching him chewing it, Liz realized that he was still hungry. She knew the meal had been meager—especially for a hungry man. But she hadn't been prepared for company that evening. Thank goodness she had an entire chocolate cake she'd made only the night before in a spur of restlessness before bedtime. She'd planned to invite Devon and Holly over to share it with her. She'd never expected that she'd be serving it to Phillip Cassidy's good-looking, though decidedly arrogant brother.

Chance's expression brightened when Liz mentioned the cake. "That sounds good," he responded immediately. She restrained a smile and gathered his plate along with her own. "I think I have some ice cream. Want some on the side?"

"Yeah, thanks."

*A man of strong appetites,* Liz thought, cutting him a slice of cake roughly three times the size of her own serving. And then she nearly choked at the unwelcome sensual images her double entendre evoked. She found herself all too curious about Chance Cassidy's approach to lovemaking. It had definitely been too long since she'd had a social life! Waiting until her blush subsided, she carried his dessert to the table. This man wasn't even her type!

The generous portion of cake and ice cream seemed to improve Chance's mood considerably. He'd eaten perhaps a third of it when he turned the conversation back to Liz's business. "So, what do you do, anyway?" he asked. "Help the brides choose their colors and their flowers?"

She resisted the impulse to sigh deeply. It was obvious that Chance had no idea of the complications involved in planning a full-scale formal wedding. His eyes widened when she began to list some of the people involved—caterers, musicians, florists, photographers, bakers, rental companies, printers, jewelers, makeup artists and hairstylists, officiants.

"It's my job to consult on all details of the wedding and then to make sure everything goes smoothly during the event," she explained. "I keep files on available locations for parties, weddings and receptions, try to stay informed on prices and new services in the area, maintain current lists of merchants and businesses for recommendation to my clients. When things go wrong,

I have to step in with last-minute replacements or substitutions."

Chance was obviously appalled at what he must have considered the unnecessary complexity of a ritual that could be so easily accomplished in the form of a nononsense, fifteen-minute civil ceremony. "How much would all that cost?" he asked bluntly.

She answered matter-of-factly, naming her most recently calculated average for a formal wedding complete with all the trimmings.

Chance choked on a bite of cake. "That's the most ridiculous thing I've ever heard!" he pronounced. "Who'd spend that kind of money for a half-hour event?"

"The weddings generally last considerably longer than a half hour," Liz pointed out in wry amusement. "There are rehearsals, dinners, receptions."

"And half of all marriages end in divorce, usually within the first few years," he added. "Sounds like a waste of money to me. With a stake like that, the couple could set up housekeeping, put a down payment on a home."

"This is my livelihood we're discussing, remember?" Liz asked lightly. "Obviously there's a demand for my services or I wouldn't be in business."

Disgusted, Chance shook his head. "Is Phillip planning to spend that kind of money?"

Because Phillip had told her that his older brother had worked very hard to put him through college, Liz swallowed an angry retort that Phillip's plans were not really any of Chance's business. "The bride's family is generally responsible for the expense of a wedding," she explained coolly.

His chin lifted defensively, as though she'd implied that he couldn't afford to provide for his brother's wedding, should he be so inclined. "In this case, the matter may prove to be hypothetical, anyway," he muttered. "Phillip is too young to be getting married in June. I think he'll understand that when I've talked to him."

"Yelled at him, you mean," Liz accused, pushing her dessert away unfinished. "You really think you have the right to interfere in Phillip and Sara's engagement?"

"Yes," he replied.

She couldn't get over his arrogance. "No wonder Phillip told you about it in a letter," she said. "He must have known this was how you'd react."

She watched his face as her barb hit home. Belatedly she wished she could recall her words. She'd suspected earlier that Chance had been hurt by his brother's letter—now she saw how deep that hurt was. Phillip had used poor judgment in choosing the easy way out; his family deserved more consideration.

Her sympathy lessened her irritation with Chance. "I understand that you're concerned about your brother."

He eyed her impassively. "Do you?"

"Of course. Don't you think Neal and I have similar concerns about Sara?"

"Then why aren't you doing anything to stop this? Looks to me like you're encouraging them."

"Because it isn't our place to interfere!" she answered heatedly. "Nor is it yours! Why do you automatically assume Phillip is making a mistake, anyway? You haven't even met Sara."

Shoving his empty dessert plate away, Chance pushed himself out of his chair and began to pace the room restlessly. "Look, it's nothing personal against your niece," he conceded. "I just think Phillip is too young to tie himself down to marriage. He's never even been serious about a woman before! And as for this plan of his to go to work for your brother..."

When he didn't immediately finish the sentence, Liz rose and placed her hands on her hips. "What about it?"

"He can forget it. Dammit, we've always agreed that he'd come to work for me when he got his degree!"

"Phillip is fascinated by Neal's software-development company," Liz explained. "Neal says Phillip hangs around the offices every chance he gets, that he shows enormous potential in the field."

Chance turned to glare over his shoulder at her. "Phillip's got a head for business, all right. With the M.B.A. he'll receive in June, he'll be an asset to any company. Mine, for example. It was always the plan that he'd take over the paperwork end of the business, leaving me free to concentrate on the construction end, which is what I'm most qualified for."

"Whose plan was that, Chance? Yours or Phillip's?"

"It was *our* plan, dammit!" he answered angrily. "I never forced it on him. He always agreed it was what he wanted—until he met your niece and her father, anyway."

"Maybe he was only saying what he thought you wanted to hear," Liz suggested, choosing her words carefully. "Maybe he didn't know what he really wanted."

"And maybe your precious niece doesn't want a husband who earns his living from something as blue-collar as the construction business," Chance returned cuttingly. "Wouldn't fit in with her country-club, vacation-condo crowd, would he?"

Liz's hands clenched to fists at her waist. "Why, you—" She paused only long enough to draw a calming breath. "My niece is *not* a snob! How dare you judge my family without even knowing them?"

Chance whirled to face her fully, his expression fierce. "Look, I've done some checking into this brother of yours. I know more about him than you might think. I'm not at all sure I want my brother mixed up with him."

Stiffening in incredulous fury, Liz gasped. "Neal is a highly respected businessman! He has an impeccable reputation, both personally and professionally. You couldn't possibly have found out anything that suggests otherwise."

"Your brother is a notoriously ruthless businessman with a reputation for unbending perfectionism and a neurotic obsession with privacy," Chance replied. "His business practices are honorable enough, but it seems that all his associates are afraid to cross him for fear of swift and merciless reprisal. He comes from an old-money background and is generally believed to be somewhat out of touch with the working class. He gives quite a bit of money to charity, but doesn't directly involve himself with any cause. Politicians fawn over him, gossip columnists repeatedly name him 'most eligible bachelor' and speculate about the personal life he's so concerned about hiding."

Liz winced, knowing that at least part of Chance's summation was accurate. "Are you telling me you run your own business any differently?" she hazarded. Something told her that Chance hadn't made a financial success of himself without maintaining rigid control over his own employees.

He cleared his throat. "I—uh—"

Her curt, humorless laugh interrupted him. "Just as I thought. Don't tell me that you and Neal aren't very much alike in business, Chance. Now that I've met you, I believe you and my brother have a great deal in common. And as far as arrogance, *you're* the one who's here to interfere in another person's life. You don't find that rather presumptuous?"

Chance crossed his arms, refusing to respond.

"I'll agree that Neal is a private person," Liz went on evenly. "He doesn't believe that just because he's wealthy and runs a large, successful business, he owes the public any details about his personal life. He's been the subject of gossip and speculation for years, and he hates that. Do you blame him?"

"Don't ask me. The society columns aren't particularly interested in running the juicy details of a carpenter's life. I find it a little hard to sympathize."

"You know who the real snob is, Chance? *You are.* A reverse snob. It's true that Neal and I come from a wealthy background, but we work as hard as you do for our money. Neal started his company without any help from our father, with only a small inheritance from our maternal grandfather. He also managed to raise his daughter while he was making a success of his company. He was a young single parent on a strict budget for the first ten years of Sara's life, so don't tell me he doesn't identify with the working class. It wasn't until our parents died a few years ago that he inherited half their estate. By that time he'd already made his own fortune with Archer Industries."

"Just whatever happened to Sara's mother, anyway?" Chance asked, curious. "That was one thing I couldn't find out about."

"Because it was none of your business," Liz replied coldly. She had no intention of telling him that Neal and Sara's mother, Lynn, had never been married. Selfish, shallow Lynn hadn't wanted the baby she and Neal had conceived, but Neal had refused to allow her to abort his child. Lynn had carried the baby to term—for a price. She'd taken off for the bright lights of the West Coast only a few weeks after Sara's birth, and hadn't been heard from since, leaving Neal to struggle to support their child after his own parents had all but disowned him for his youthful mistake. They didn't go quite that far, but they rarely saw or spoke to their son for the remainder of their lives.

The elder Archers had been bitterly disappointed that their heir, their hope for a brilliant political future, had "ruined his life" by taking responsibility for a child they would have swept from their lives without a second thought. Liz, who'd been only twelve when Sara was born, had stood by Neal, spending every moment she could with him and the baby—loving them with the intensity that she simply could not feel for her stern, unbending, harshly demanding parents.

No, Liz wouldn't try to explain Sara's existence to Chance, who would probably use Sara's illegitimacy as just another reason she shouldn't be marrying into his family. As far as Liz was concerned, Sara was a precious gift who had been sent to enrich their lives. Neal had often expressed the same sentiment. Chance Cassidy should be grateful that his brother had been fortunate enough to meet and fall in love with Sara Archer.

"I think you'd better leave now, Chance. It seems you already have your mind made up about the Archer family and nothing I can say will change it."

Chance sighed and shoved a hand through his hair. "Look, it's nothing personal, okay? I'm sure your family is very nice. But I still plan to do anything I can to prevent my brother from ruining his life."

He couldn't have chosen a more unfortunate phrasing if he'd deliberately tried to remind Liz of her overbearing parents. "What you will probably succeed in doing," Liz warned, "is alienating your brother forever. I've gotten to know Phillip quite well during the past few months, Chance. He's a very determined young man, and he is deeply in love with my niece. You'll be making a big mistake if you make him choose between her and you. Believe me, I know from experience that family relationships can be permanently damaged by that sort of ultimatum."

"I think I know my brother better than you do," Chance replied defensively.

She eyed him impassively. "I suppose that remains to be seen. Good night, Chance."

He winced at her tone. "I guess I didn't handle this very well."

"You might want to use a bit more tact when you talk to Phillip," she agreed. She quickly retrieved his jacket from her bedroom, then stalked to the front door. "Good night, Chance," she repeated, wanting him to leave before they got into another quarrel about their respective families.

Exhaling deeply, he reached for his jacket. "Thanks for the dinner."

"You're welcome." She opened the door.

Resignedly, he sauntered past her, pausing with one hand on the door to keep her from closing it in his face. "We'll see each other again," he murmured, his narrowed gaze locking with hers.

She resisted the urge to swallow. "Perhaps," she said coolly.

His smile was enigmatic. "Count on it." The words held a promise—or had it been a warning? Liz closed the door behind him.

Suddenly exhausted, she cleaned the kitchen quickly. She was still trying to figure out Chance Cassidy hours later as she lay sleeplessly in her bed.

Why was she was so inexplicably attracted to him—despite her irritation with him and despite the unpleasant similarities she saw between him and her insufferably domineering parents and ex-husband?

# 3

LIZ HAD HOPED TO SLEEP in the next morning—
Thanksgiving Day. She wasn't pleased to be awakened
very early by an imperious knocking on the door.
Stumbling out of bed, she pushed her hair out of her
face and reached for her thick terry robe. Since she'd
received no call from the security desk downstairs, she
assumed Mrs. O'Hara next door was out of coffee
again. She didn't mind loaning the coffee, since Mrs.
O'Hara always paid back what she borrowed, but she
really wished the woman would check her supplies *the
night before!*

She opened the door only to stare in astonishment at
the man facing her from the hallway. "Chance! What—
How did you get past the security desk?"

"I hate to tell you this," he drawled, "but the security
in this building isn't that great. More for show than for
real, I'm afraid. The guy went off to the bathroom, and
I walked into the elevator. May I come in?"

She was going to make an irate call to the apartment
manager immediately after Chance's departure. She
was paying exorbitant rent for that so-called security!
Reluctantly she moved aside to allow him to enter. "I
wasn't expecting to see you today," she said, though she

knew her words were unnecessary. It was quite obvious that he knew he'd taken her by surprise.

"I've been thinking about what you said last night," he admitted, turning in the middle of the room to face her. He was wearing the leather jacket again, with a pale blue shirt and clean jeans. His crisp brown hair was carelessly wind-tossed, his eyes shadowed as if from a near-sleepless night. He looked much like a man on the verge of a confession.

Liz eyed him suspiciously, not at all sure she trusted his sheepish pose, despite the unwelcome attraction she felt at seeing him again. "I said several things last night," she reminded. "What, in particular, have you been thinking about?"

"You warned me that I may lose my brother if I handle this situation badly. I don't want to lose my brother."

Liz studied his set face hopefully. "Does that mean you're not going to object to his engagement now?"

Chance hesitated, then shook his head slowly. "It means I'm here to ask you to help me."

Liz sighed. "You never give up, do you?"

"Not when it's important," he said grimly. "Will you help me?"

"Look, I know you're concerned about your brother. I understand," she told him. "But you have no right— *we* have no right—to interfere with his plans. Why can't you see that?"

"You really think your niece and my brother are old enough to handle the demands of marriage now?" he asked.

"I—" Liz ran a hand through her unbrushed hair and sighed again. "I don't know, Chance. Sara's so young— and so is Phillip, really. They're just starting out, they have careers to build, neither of them has had much experience in life. I married young myself—carried away by romantic fantasies that shattered very soon after they were confronted by reality."

"You *do* think they're too young," Chance observed in a satisfied tone.

"It doesn't matter what I think," she reminded him in exasperation. "They're adults. And they're very much in love. If any young couple has a chance, I think Sara and Phillip do. I won't interfere."

"You don't have to help them along by organizing the damned wedding," Chance accused.

"If I don't, someone else will," Liz pointed out logically. "Sara's not going to let something that minor stop her plans. She'd be hurt, angry with me, but she'd hire someone else. Or do it herself. She's worked with me often in the past. She's quite capable of organizing her own wedding."

"Then what *can* we do?" Chance questioned, looking at her in a way that made her think he was a man who hadn't often asked for help.

"Nothing," she replied simply.

He looked away with a scowl. "Dammit, there must be something."

"Not without tearing apart your family—and possibly mine," she asserted. "And I'm not going to risk that, Chance. I can't believe you would."

He didn't answer.

Feeling his tension, Liz carefully stepped closer. "You've been responsible for Phillip for a long time, haven't you?"

"Since he was just a kid."

"You're going to have to let him grow up sometime. You know that, don't you?"

Again, he remained stubbornly silent.

Liz bit her lip, knowing there was little more she could say. Chance would have to struggle in his own way to accept Phillip's right to make his own decisions—no matter how much Chance disapproved of those decisions.

"Maybe you'll feel better about the situation once you meet Sara and Neal," she suggested quietly. "Sara's really a very sweet young woman, bright and loving. And Neal's a good man—quiet, but nice. Not nearly the ogre you've apparently envisioned after listening to gossip about him."

"I never listen to gossip," Chance retorted.

She lifted a skeptical eyebrow, remembering the things he'd told her about Neal the night before.

He grimaced. "Well, not often."

"Then you'll meet them with an open mind?" she prodded.

"I'll try," he said reluctantly. He shoved his hands into the pockets of his jacket. "I know it's Thanksgiving— I suppose you have plans for dinner?"

"I'm working today. I have a wedding this evening. It will take me all day to get ready for it."

"I see."

"What about you? Will you be going back to Birmingham today?"

"I'm not sure when I'm going home," he admitted. "I'd like to talk to you a bit more about your family. I want to be well prepared when I finally catch up with Phillip. Maybe we could have dinner tomorrow?"

She was startled that he wasn't planning to leave immediately, though, to be honest, she was oddly pleased that he wasn't. Her feelings about Chance Cassidy were decidedly mixed. But what would he do with himself today, alone on Thanksgiving in a strange town? Too bad she wouldn't have time to at least have dinner with him, but she simply couldn't neglect her duties involving the huge wedding she'd arranged for her clients this evening.

"Of course, I'll have dinner with you tomorrow, if you choose to stay," she told him gently. "But I won't change my mind about helping you end Sara's engagement, Chance."

He shrugged off the warning, then said abruptly, "Look, if you talk to your brother or niece today, I'd appreciate it if you don't tell them you've seen me. I don't want Phillip to know yet that I've come to Atlanta."

Though reluctant to deceive her family, Liz agreed to his request. She didn't want to ruin the family's vacation.

Chance looked toward the door. "Guess I'd better go." He didn't sound particularly enthusiastic about leaving.

Liz wondered why she wasn't more anxious for him to be gone. "Yes. I suppose you'd better. I have to get dressed," she forced herself to say briskly.

He lowered his gaze, taking in her loosely belted robe. Though the garment was thick and decently voluminous, Liz still felt a strange urge to draw it more closely around her—as if Chance could see through it to the sheer silk she wore beneath.

Their eyes met for a long moment, and then Chance was gone without another word. Liz locked her door behind him, noticing with surprise that her hand wasn't quite steady.

She never got around to calling the apartment manager to complain about the failure in "security."

"HI, MOTHER. It's Chance. Happy Thanksgiving."

"Happy Thanksgiving to you, too, dear. I miss you. I miss having both my boys with me today. Have you— have you talked to Phillip?"

Chance sighed, cradling the receiver of the pay phone against his ear, straining to hear over the sounds of traffic from the highway behind him. He'd stopped at a phone stand outside a convenience store to let his stepmother know about his impulsive plan to spend another day or two in Atlanta, even though Phillip wasn't even there. "Phillip's out of the state, Mother. In Florida. I have a feeling he'll be calling you later to wish you happy Thanksgiving. Do me a favor, will you?"

"What favor, Chance?"

"Don't tell him I'm in Atlanta, will you? I'm checking into the background of Neal Archer and I really don't want Phillip to know until I'm ready to tell him. Will you do that for me, Mother?"

"But what should I tell him if he asks to speak to you?"

"Trust me. He won't." Chance was certain of that. Having sent a letter announcing his plans, Phillip would avoid Chance for as long as possible, knowing a confrontation was inevitable. Phillip would call his mother on Thanksgiving, but would merely ask Nadine to pass along a greeting to Chance.

"When will you be home?"

"I'm not sure yet. I'll let you know. You'll be okay, won't you?"

"Of course. Martha's taking good care of me, as always. But I do miss you."

"I miss you, too. I'll keep in touch."

"Please do. And be careful, dear."

"I will. Bye, Mother."

Replacing the receiver, Chance brushed his hair off his forehead and turned toward his truck. He really couldn't have explained why he wasn't on his way back to Birmingham. He strongly suspected that Elizabeth Archer had something to do with his decision to stay in Atlanta a while longer.

*"Idiot,"* he muttered, crawling behind the wheel.

AS BUSY AS THE DAY WAS, as all wedding days were, while Liz worked she pictured Chance eating Thanksgiving dinner in an out-of-the-way little diner. She didn't think he'd choose to dine alone in a nice restaurant; truck stops and waffle houses seemed more his style. And more than once during the day she found herself remembering the pain in his eyes when he'd talked about the letter Phillip had sent him. Realizing that she was actually starting to sympathize with the man, she warned herself that she'd better be very careful.

It was late when she returned home. Her feet were throbbing from hours in heels; her neck and shoulders were stiff from the tension that always accompanied a formal wedding—tension that had eased somewhat when the ceremony had gone flawlessly, right down to the second arch of sabers outside the church. A few minor problems had occurred at the reception, but Liz had handled them so competently, none of the guests were even aware of them.

Normally she would be quietly content after a successful wedding. Tonight, all she could think about was Chance Cassidy. Where had he eaten? Where was he staying? Had he found companionship for the holiday evening? Why did it matter if he had?

She reminded herself of her loyalty to Sara, her determination to protect her niece from Chance's heavy-handed interference in their plans. Again she reminded herself that domineering men didn't interest her, that she'd learned the hard way that such men were all wrong for her. She told herself that Chance had given her no indication that he was interested in her as anything other than Sara's potentially useful aunt. None of that seemed to matter, however.

As she finally and restlessly drifted to sleep, she was remembering the way his intent gaze had seemed to penetrate her robe. She pictured again the flicker of thoroughly masculine response she'd seen in his eyes before he'd left, and remembered the answering shiver that had coursed down her spine.

Chance Cassidy could prove to be a problem in more ways than one.

LIZ HAD GIVEN HER secretary the day after Thanksgiving off, for a well-deserved four-day weekend. She went to the office, though she hadn't scheduled any appointments for that day, planning to use the time to catch up on the piles of paperwork.

She wasn't particularly surprised to look up at midmorning to find Chance leaning against the open doorway of her office. The man was making a habit of appearing unexpectedly. "Here to twist my arm a bit more?" she asked dryly.

He grinned. "Maybe. Going to throw me out?"

His rare, flashing smile did amazing things to his face. She cleared her throat. "Since you're bigger than I am, I think that might be a bit difficult."

"I'll go if you ask me to." The smile had vanished as his expression became serious. She could tell that he meant what he said; all she'd have to do was ask and he'd be gone.

"There's a fresh pot of coffee in the supply room, if you'd like a cup," she heard herself saying instead.

Chance looked as though she'd surprised him almost as much as she had herself, but didn't question her invitation. He disappeared for a few minutes to return with a foam cup of coffee in one hand. "Doing paperwork?" he asked, nodding toward the littered desk in front of her.

She made a face and motioned for him to be seated. "Yes. A necessary evil, isn't it?"

Chance grimaced expressively. "It's a pain in the butt," he stated less delicately. "I hate it. Phillip is—" He paused with a scowl. "Phillip *was* going to take over that end of my business for me once he got his M.B.A."

Liz studied him meditatively. "Does it bother you more that Phillip's planning to be married, Chance, or that he's accepted a job with my brother?"

"Phillip belongs with me. I need him, dammit. I'm good—damned good—at the construction end of things, but the rest of it requires someone with a strong business education. I've only got a few hours of college credit. I've counted on Phillip to join me when he graduates. I can't believe he'd let me down like this without a lot of pressure from someone."

"From Sara, you mean?"

"She'd be my first guess," he agreed coolly.

Rather than defend her niece again, Liz employed another tactic. "Phillip tells us that you've been very successful with your company. According to him, you started small and you've built it into a well-known, well-respected construction firm. He says you've grabbed some of the largest contracts in the Birmingham area lately. Sounds to me like you're perfectly capable of running the company on your own."

Chance actually looked embarrassed. "I do okay for someone who started out driving nails on a construction crew," he conceded gruffly. "But Phillip's the one who knows computers and numbers and market trends and all that garbage. Hell, he's been reading the *Wall Street Journal* since he was in junior high. He asked for a subscription as a Christmas gift when he was a senior. I still don't have a subscription for myself. Wouldn't have time to read it if I did."

Liz thought it was fairly clear that Chance felt over-shadowed by his bright, ambitious younger brother. Mistakenly, of course. She could try convincing him that it required even more savvy and ambition to come up the hard way—from driving nails on a construction crew—than it did through an M.B.A. program.

He didn't give her an opportunity. Pointing to the papers spread out in front of her, he asked, "Tell me more about your business. It amazes me how compli-cated you made it sound last night."

Because it still piqued that he'd so greatly under-estimated her work, she complied, outlining the func-tions of Special Events, Inc. Chance listened intently, occasionally asking questions, twice shaking his head in amazement.

Neither of them mentioned his leaving, as though it were perfectly natural for him to be hanging out at her office while she worked. An hour and a half later, Liz looked up from her paperwork to find Chance en-grossed in the planner from the wedding she'd orga-nized the night before. He intercepted her look, smiled, and then continued studying it. With a small smile, Liz returned to work, surprisingly content with his quiet companionship.

As they sat, her telephone rang three times. Liz han-dled each call briskly, professionally. The fourth call made her look up at Chance with a frown—their pleasant interlude was to be disturbed. "Hello, Sara," she said.

Chance's head went up sharply. He made a quick gesture Liz knew was a reminder that she wasn't to mention him during the call. She chewed her lower lip in indecision, torn between her loyalty to her family and her reluctance to initiate the unavoidable conflict just yet.

"What are you doing at the office today?" Sara demanded sternly. "Don't you know most people take the day after Thanksgiving off for a long weekend? Particularly when they worked through the holiday itself?" she added. "I tried calling you twice yesterday to wish you happy Thanksgiving and missed you both times."

"I know. I got your messages on the machine. Thanks for calling. Are you and Neal and Phillip having a nice time?"

"Wonderful. I wish you could have come with us, Aunt Liz. Daddy and Phillip are getting along great."

"That's—um—nice," Liz remarked awkwardly, glad that Chance couldn't overhear the conversation, though he kept his eyes on her face as she spoke.

"You should hear them talking business. Daddy says Phillip has an amazing grasp of the business world and will be an invaluable asset to his company. Isn't that exciting? I mean, after all, Daddy doesn't say things like that unless he really means them, does he?"

"No. He certainly doesn't."

"And Phillip can't wait to join Archer Industries. He's a little worried about his brother's reaction—the two of them had discussed Phillip moving back to Bir-

mingham and joining his brother's firm. I'm sure
Chance will understand when Phillip explains how
badly he wants to get into the electronics industry. At
least, I hope he'll understand. I haven't met Chance, of
course, but he sounds rather intimidating. He's the only
person I can think of who can make Phillip nervous."

Phillip wasn't the only one unnerved by the intimidating Chance Cassidy, Liz thought, shifting restlessly
in her seat as Chance continued to watch her. And what
was she supposed to say now, anyway? She didn't want
Chance to know Sara was talking about him!

Fortunately, Sara didn't dwell long on the subject.

"Anyway," Sara chattered on, "I just wanted to call
and say hi and tell you how much we miss you. You're
not working too hard, I hope."

"No, I'm—"

"Good. Love you, Aunt Liz."

"I love you, too, sweetie."

"I have to go. Phillip and I are going to a dinner theater tonight. Daddy's got a hot chess game planned
with an old retired guy from one of the other condos.
Honestly, Aunt Liz, we have to find him a woman! I
think he and Devon would be a great match, don't you?
We'll talk about it more when I get home, okay?"

"Bye, Sara. Give Neal and Phillip my love."

"I will. See you Monday!"

Monday. Liz hung up the phone. Sara had sounded
so happy. Liz couldn't bear to think that such happiness could be shattered so soon. "I don't want you to

hurt her, Chance," she said, slowly raising her eyes to his.

"I don't want to hurt her," he assured her grimly. "I just want what's best for my brother."

"For your brother?" she repeated with a trace of bitterness. "Or for you?"

He scowled. "That's rather low, isn't it?"

"I don't know. I only know that my niece is happier now than I've ever seen her. And you're the one threatening her happiness. Do you expect me to welcome you with open arms?" she exclaimed.

He half shrugged. "It would have been nice," he murmured unexpectedly, his gaze briefly sweeping her body.

Liz caught her breath at the unmistakable sexual innuendo. It was the first time he'd acknowledged such an attraction. She'd half believed that she was the only one who felt it—though somehow she'd suspected from the beginning that the feeling was mutual.

Without waiting for her to stumble around for an answer, Chance set aside the wedding planner and quickly rose from his chair, reaching for the leather jacket he'd tossed over the back of it. "I'll let you get back to work now," he said, putting on his jacket. "I'll pick you up at your place at seven."

"That's right. I said I'd have dinner with you, didn't I?" she muttered, unable to back out now—and not sure she would if she could.

"Dinner, maybe a movie. You know—a date?"

"You mean another evening to argue about Sara and Phillip's plans," she corrected warily, uncomfortable with his choice of description.

What was it about his rare smiles that completely disarmed her? He gave her one now, making her knees so weak, she was glad she was sitting down. "No," he said quietly. "I mean a date. See you at seven."

She told herself that she wasn't at all charmed by his arrogant assumption that she wanted to go out with him. She told herself his approach had been clumsy, utterly lacking in courtesy. The men she knew, the men she dated, would never *tell* her when they'd pick her up! They'd *ask* for a date, not inform her she was going on one. It would serve Chance Cassidy right if she weren't home at seven—if she found something else to do for the evening.

But even as the thought crossed her mind, she knew she wouldn't follow through with it. She'd be at her door at seven, dressed to go out with him. Oh, she'd tell him what she thought of his arrogance, let him know quite clearly that such behavior would get him no-where with *this* particular woman. She'd go out with him, anyway. Just because she wanted to be with him.

*Trouble.* Chance Cassidy was definitely trouble. Yet, no matter how many times she reminded herself of that undeniable fact, she was prepared to throw herself right into trouble's path—perhaps right into his arms.

# 4

LIZ PREPARED HER SPEECH while waiting for Chance that evening. She knew exactly what she wanted to say to express her displeasure at his way of "asking" her for a date. She'd even rehearsed as she dressed in a floral skirt and pink silk blouse, then applied her makeup.

Unfortunately her carefully chosen words fled her mind the second she opened the door to find him standing there, giving her The Smile and holding out a small bouquet of colorful, exotic flowers that appeared to have been carefully selected to match the decor of her living room.

It seemed very much out of character for Chance to arrive bearing flowers. The faintest flush of color on his lean cheeks indicated that he was rather embarrassed by the gesture. "It occurred to me," he said in a gruff tone, "that I was a bit arrogant at your office earlier. It would have served me right if you'd stood me up. I'm glad you didn't."

*Well, hell!* He'd just totally ruined her speech by making it first. She reached for the bouquet. Their hands touched. Liz's cheeks flooded with heat. She managed to smile weakly. "Thank you for the flowers, Chance."

"You're welcome." What might have been faint satisfaction shone for a moment in his eyes. Ignoring it, she
turned away to put the flowers in water.

Several times during the evening, Liz wished that she
and Chance had met a year earlier—before Sara and
Phillip had met—so she could simply enjoy him without a constant awareness of his underlying purpose for
being with her. Regardless of that purpose—of his un-
justified antipathy toward her family and his determination to end his brother's engagement to her niece—
Liz couldn't help liking him.

As if by unspoken agreement, they didn't talk about
their families. They both enjoyed the movie they selected, discussing it afterward at a casual, out-of-the-
way restaurant that was one of her favorites. During the
meal, Liz discovered that Chance could actually be
quite charming when he dropped the large chip on his
shoulder. Quite charming, indeed.

He was easy to be with. He displayed none of the self-
conscious posturing that so irritated her in many of the
executives she'd dated over the past few years. Nor did
he have the need to impress her with his money or his
accomplishments. He was amusing, in a dry, laconic
way, particularly when he related his adventures at a
coin-operated laundry that afternoon, where he'd
washed the few changes of clothing he'd brought with
him to Atlanta.

Though he didn't say a lot, Liz reflected with a secret
smile, what he said was always interesting.

If only...

Chance was almost smugly pleased with the way the evening was proceeding. Intercepting a few envious looks from less fortunate men in the restaurant, he felt a surge of pride to be with the woman who sat across the table from him. Chance Cassidy, carpenter and businessman, son of a plumber, grandson of a second-generation milkman, was on a date with a beautiful, elegant, very classy woman. Not only that, but they were getting along great.

Chance wasn't usually comfortable with beautiful, elegant, classy women, usually feeling prickly and defensive in their presence. But Liz was different, somehow. Her eyes were warm when they rested on his face, her smile lovely. Too bad about that other business between them. And he was aware of her lingering wariness, the guardedness in her expression on those occasions when one or the other slipped and mentioned their families.

Chance's satisfaction was rudely shattered when a vaguely familiar-looking blond man in his mid-thirties stopped to greet Liz with an enthusiastic kiss. Right on the mouth. A kiss she returned all too readily, Chance noted with a scowl.

"You look beautiful, as always, Elizabeth," he said in a cultured, British accent. "What are you doing in town? I thought you'd be in Florida with the rest of the family."

"No such luck," Liz replied lightly, smiling at the guy with so much affection that Chance's fist automatically clenched in his lap. "This member of the Archer family has to work this weekend. But I hope you're planning to get some rest while you're home, Tristan. You look awful. Did you have to check those bags under your eyes when you flew in?"

"Cruel, Elizabeth. Very cruel," he chided her. And then he glanced across the table to Chance, who looked narrowly back at him. "Who's your dangerous-looking friend?"

Liz made a futile effort to stifle a quick laugh. "Chance Cassidy, this is Tristan Parrish. An old friend of the family," she added.

Parrish winced at her wording. "Not that old."

Chance just managed to conceal his own distaste. No wonder the guy had looked familiar: Anyone who regularly watched cable news would recognize Tristan Parrish, the award-winning reporter with a reputation for being both reckless and persistent in his pursuit of a story—and women. During the Gulf War, the supermarket rags had dubbed him "The Desert Dish"—to Parrish's alleged chagrin.

Unable to force himself to lie that it was nice meeting him, Chance only nodded in response to the introduction, wondering all the while whether Liz and Tristan were more than just "old friends."

"Cassidy," Tristan repeated. "Any relation to that nice young man Sara's gotten herself engaged to marry?"

"Phillip is my brother," Chance supplied curtly.

"I see. Then you're getting a delightful sister-in-law. I've known Sara since she was a child. She's a treasure."

"I haven't met her yet."

"No?" Tristan looked surprised.

"Chance is afraid that Phillip and Sara are too young to get married," Liz spoke up. She glanced from Chance to Tristan.

"They are young," Tristan agreed, immediately defensive for his friends, "but adults nonetheless."

Chance didn't particularly like the man's proprietorial air toward Sara. Exactly how close was he to the Archer family? And to Liz, in particular?

"We shouldn't keep you here, Tristan," Liz said. "I'm sure you have a lovely brunette waiting breathlessly at a table for you."

"Redhead, love. But you're right, I should get back. I expect we'll see each other again, Cassidy."

"Maybe we will," Chance agreed vaguely, knowing Tristan referred to the wedding Chance still hoped wouldn't take place. Neither made any effort to shake hands.

Liz waited only until Tristan was out of hearing before glaring at Chance. "Are you determined to dislike anyone associated with the Archer family without even giving them the benefit of a doubt, Chance?"

"I don't know what you mean," he muttered, not meeting her eyes.

"You recognized Tristan?"

He nodded. "TV reporter."

"You have something against reporters?"

Chance shrugged. "Haven't really dealt with that many of them."

"You were very cool to Tristan. Some might even have called your behavior rude. Do you have something against Tristan personally? Or is it only his friendship with Neal that bothers you?"

"Actually, I was more concerned about his friendship with you," Chance responded with calculated coolness.

Liz was silent, her surprise evident. "With me?" she repeated after a moment.

He nodded, watching closely to gauge her reaction. "Why?"

"Do I really have to spell it out for you?"

Her cheeks flushed. That was one of the things that attracted him to her. It was obviously difficult for her to hide her emotions. She had an honest face. Honesty was a trait he considered very important in a woman.

She busied herself by looking down at her nearly empty plate. "I thought you wanted to talk about Sara and Phillip," she murmured.

"We did talk about them," he reminded her. "You're not going to change your mind and help me convince them to cancel, or at least postpone, this wedding?"

"No," she declared. "I won't risk my relationship with my niece."

"So I'll just have to handle my brother as I think best."

She eyed him warily. "Yes, I suppose so."

"Then there's no need for us to discuss it any further, is there?"

"No, I—suppose not."

He held her gaze with his and smiled faintly. "Guess we'll just have to find something else to talk about, won't we?"

Liz cleared her throat. "Hasn't the weather been nice this weekend?"

Chance threw his head back and laughed at her desperately lame attempt at making safe conversation. It was the first time he'd really felt like laughing since Phillip's letter had arrived a week earlier.

Again Liz found Chance's smile much too appealing. His deep, rich laugh was irresistible. Chance Cassidy was definitely going to be more trouble than she'd originally suspected.

LATER LIZ RATIONALIZED that she'd only invited him in for coffee to discover what his plans were for the remainder of the weekend. For Sara's sake, of course.

"Where are you staying, Chance?" she asked when she handed him his coffee cup and settled on the sofa beside him.

He grimaced and named a hotel. "Oh, no!" she exclaimed. "That's a terrible place. I should have recommended something to you when you arrived."

He shook his head. "I was tired enough Wednesday night to bunk down in the first hotel with a vacancy. I checked out this afternoon. Thought I'd try to find someplace a little cleaner for the next two nights. Any suggestions?"

"I hope there are some vacancies this late," she fretted. "After all, it is a holiday weekend."

He set his coffee cup on a coaster on the low oval table in front of the couch. "Don't worry about it. I'll find something."

Torn by indecision, she chewed on her lower lip. "I suppose you *could* stay here tonight," she suggested hesitantly. "The couch is a hideaway bed." She assumed he'd be heading back for Birmingham the next day. Surely it was only polite to offer him a place to stay for the night.

He faced her, his expression unreadable. "If I stay here," he said slowly, "I wouldn't want to sleep on the couch."

"If you stay here," she answered crisply, "you *will* sleep on the couch. I'm not in the habit of inviting men I barely know to share my bed."

"Then I'll just have to see that you get to know me better, won't I?" he murmured, and reached for her.

Chance may have been a bit rough around the edges socially, but his kiss was skilled, igniting sensations Liz hadn't experienced in years. She resisted only a moment before responding, softening her lips to part beneath his.

There had been something about this man that had drawn her from the moment she'd seen him standing in her reception area, looking so out of place in her pink-chintz-and-ruffles office. Something in his eyes, something in his smile, melted her defenses. Now his kiss spoke to her of pleasures only imagined before, of a passion that went beyond anything she'd known with any other man.

It was quite a long time before she could pull away from him. She placed one trembling hand on his shoulder as her lips slowly parted from his. Still close enough that she could feel his breath on her cheek, she looked into his eyes. "I can't do this, Chance," she whispered huskily. "Casual sex just isn't right for me."

"Whatever else it may be," he replied, his own voice rather hoarse, "it wouldn't be casual."

She swallowed. "Chance—"

"I'll sleep on the couch, Liz," he told her, releasing her abruptly. "But do me a favor—lock your bedroom door."

She did. But she was rather surprised at how hard it was to make herself do it.

CHANCE STOOD BY the oversize window in Liz's living room, the tangled bedclothes on the fold-down sofa behind him testimony to his inability to sleep. It was after one in the morning and he was tired, but the memory of kissing Liz had him pacing the floor, aching with need.

He wanted her.

He'd wanted other women, had had his share of them. But he couldn't remember ever aching quite this fiercely for any particular woman.

What was it about her? he asked himself for—well, he'd lost track of the number of times he'd pondered the question. He couldn't picture himself having a good time with her on one of his favorite kinds of weekend outings—camping, fishing, hiking, the outdoor sports he enjoyed so much. She'd probably bitch the whole time about her hair, her nails, her sweat-streaked makeup.

He'd heard it all before—one weekend when he'd made the mistake of taking a sexy redhead into the mountains with him. He and Dani had had some good times before that weekend, and he'd never seen her again afterward—by mutual choice. And Dani hadn't been half as sleek and sophisticated as Elizabeth Archer, with her old-money poise and aplomb.

Still, the passion he'd felt in her kisses had startled him. Pleasantly. Would she respond so eagerly in bed? And the images of her in bed with him had him pacing her living-room floor, his gaze turning repeatedly to the bedroom door that was all that separated her from him.

He really should put a stop to this, he told himself sternly. Even if he and Liz began an affair, the awkward connection between their families would surely result in a messy conclusion. He had to remember that his primary purpose for being here was to prevent his younger brother from jumping into marriage and destroying his long-held plans for Cassidy Construction Company.

So why was he still in Atlanta two days after discovering that Phillip was in Florida? The truth was, after taking one look at Liz, he hadn't been in a hurry to return to Birmingham. And Phillip didn't have a damned thing to do with Chance's fascination with Liz.

"Damn," Chance muttered, glaring at the closed bedroom door. "This could get more complicated than I'd expected."

LIZ MADE CERTAIN that she was fully dressed before stepping out of her bedroom Saturday morning. After belting her blue floral dress, she paused in front of the mirror to pat a few stray hairs into her prim upsweep. She winced at her reflection, noting the faint signs of a restless night, hoping Chance wouldn't spot them. She'd been much too conscious of him close by to sleep comfortably, and she wouldn't want him to guess how tempted she'd been to open her door to him.

She couldn't understand her own reactions to Chance. Desire? Not so surprising, perhaps. He was virile, and it had been a long time since she'd given in to her usually manageable sexual needs. Maybe she shouldn't be so concerned that he'd made her want him so easily. But, for some reason, she felt there was more to it than sexual attraction. And it was that "more" that made her nervous as she opened her door and stepped out in search of him.

The sheets, blanket and pillow were neatly stacked on the end of the couch, which he'd already folded back. A battered pair of boots lay on the floor beside one of the armchairs. Chance wasn't in the room, nor was the overnight bag he'd brought in from his car last night while she'd gathered the linens for the hideaway bed. She could hear him moving around in the guest bathroom. Grateful for the extra few moments' delay before having to face him again, she headed for the kitchen. She didn't usually have breakfast, but she suspected Chance would be hungry. And this time she'd prepare enough food to satisfy him.

Drawn by the aroma of brewing coffee and frying bacon, Chance appeared in the kitchen doorway a few minutes later, tucking his clean white shirt into the waistband of a freshly washed pair of well-worn jeans. She smiled as she remembered his humorous account of struggling with an ancient, recalcitrant washing machine at a laundromat the afternoon before. "Good morning, Chance."

"Morning. That smells good. I'm starved," he announced.

"Pour yourself a cup of coffee and have a seat. Your breakfast will be ready in just a minute."

"You didn't have to do this, but thanks."

She concentrated on the crisping bacon. "You're welcome," she murmured self-consciously.

The kitchen seemed unusually small as Chance poured himself a cup of coffee and accidentally brushed against her as he moved to the small kitchen table. Or had it been an accident?

"How did you sleep?" he asked casually, his chair scraping lightly against the tile floor when he pulled it away from the table.

"Fine," she lied. "And you?"

He grunted an incoherent reply that made her believe he hadn't slept any better than she had.

"You look nice today," he commented after a brief pause. "Do you always dress like this on Saturdays, or is it for my benefit?"

"I'm working today. There's a wedding this afternoon."

"You work every weekend?"

"Most of them," she admitted. "When I'm not doing weddings, I occasionally organize other formal affairs—parties, receptions, bar mitzvahs. I usually get that sort of job through word-of-mouth advertising."

"You're doing quite well for yourself, aren't you?"

"I try," she answered lightly, turning toward the table with his breakfast. "The biscuits should be ready to come out of the oven in—" She broke off with a smile when the oven timer chimed. "Right now."

Chance ate with an enthusiasm that Liz found rather endearing while she sipped her coffee and nibbled at a hot, jam-spread biscuit. "This is great," he told her, helping himself to a third biscuit. "First biscuits I've had in a long time that didn't come out of a can."

"Do you have someone to cook for you and your stepmother?" she asked, curious about Chance's home life.

He shrugged. "We have a live-in who takes care of Nadine—the woman who's staying with her this weekend. She's an adequate cook. On her days off, I handle the meals."

That surprised her. "Really?"

He gave her an amused look. "You didn't think I could cook?"

"No," she admitted, remembering that her ex-husband wouldn't have been caught dead in a kitchen.

Maybe she needed to stop comparing Chance to Jim.

"So what are you going to do with yourself today?" she asked when the last scrap of food was gone. "Are you going back to Birmingham?"

Chance didn't answer as he carried his plate and utensils to the sink to rinse them before stacking them in the dishwasher. "You wouldn't need an able-bodied assistant today, would you?"

She nearly choked on her last sip of coffee. "You want to help me with a wedding?"

"Well, I don't really have anything else to do at home for the remainder of the weekend—and I'd like to see you at work."

"Why?"

"Everything about you interests me," he answered simply.

She shouldn't have asked, she told herself. She should have known he'd come up with an answer like that—one she didn't know how to acknowledge.

Taking her silence as a refusal, he shrugged. "I guess I'd be in the way."

"No," she heard herself say. "You wouldn't. You're welcome to tag along—if you really want to."

He smiled, with the by-now-predictable effect on Liz's pulse. "I'd like that."

She made an effort to return the smile—and hoped very much that she wasn't making a mistake by encouraging Chance Cassidy's interest in her. A twinge of doubt nagged at her. How much of that interest was a direct result of his determination to end Phillip and Sara's engagement?

"HEY, LIZ. When did you hire the hunky assistant?" Holly asked. They were alone in the ballroom after the small beautiful wedding that Holly had photographed.

"Chance is Phillip Cassidy's brother," she explained. "He's sort of hanging around with me this weekend. He arrived Wednesday, not realizing that Phillip had left for Florida."

Holly grinned. "Guess you really hate having to entertain him. The man is certainly easy on the eyes, isn't he?"

"He's—very attractive," Liz admitted cautiously.

"Let's see. He's your brother's future son-in-law's brother. What does that make him to you? A nephew-in-law?"

Liz rolled her eyes. "If it's left up to him, he won't be *anything* to me," she replied flatly. "Chance is strongly opposed to the wedding. He thinks Phillip and Sara are too young and he plans to talk them out of it."

Holly sobered. "Oh, he does, does he? I take it he doesn't know Sara very well?"

"He doesn't know Sara at all. Phillip hasn't introduced them yet. Phillip really hasn't handled his family very well during this, Holly. I feel rather sorry for Chance and Phillip's mother," Liz admitted.

"That still doesn't give Chance the right to just show up here, expecting to put an end to the engagement," Holly argued with a toss of her red head. "And why are you on his side? Don't you know how devastated poor Sara will be by this? You know how she hates family conflicts. And she was so happy Tuesday when she announced her engagement to us!"

"Yes, I know," Liz answered. "And I'm not on Chance's side, Holly. It's just—well, I know how much Phillip hurt him, whether intentionally or not. And I don't want to see anyone hurt by this engagement—not my family or Phillip's."

"So what are you going to do about it?"

Liz sighed. "I've tried to warn Chance that he's only going to alienate them, but he's determined to interfere. Sara isn't the only stubborn one."

"Maybe you have another weapon to use. I don't think ending his brother's engagement is the only thing on the man's mind," Holly commented, her impish smile slowly returning. "He's been watching you with a very interesting look in his eyes."

"He's trying to bring me around to his side," Liz said lightly. "He wants me to help him talk Sara and Phillip into postponing their wedding. I've told him that I have no intention of helping him, of course, but I'm not sure he's given up on persuading me."

"Mmm," Holly murmured speculatively. "I don't know, Liz. He didn't look like he was thinking of his kid brother when I caught him watching you earlier. And you weren't looking at him like chopped liver, for that matter."

Liz cleared her throat. "Holly," she began, only to be interrupted by Chance's return from the parking lot, where he had gone to stow some items in Liz's car.

"Anything else to go out?" he asked helpfully.

"No, that's all." Liz tugged Holly a bit closer. "Chance, this is my friend Holly Baldwin."

Holly was treated to one of Chance's rare, potent smiles. Liz noted that the effect wasn't lost on her friend. "Nice to meet you, Holly," he said politely. "I watched you at work. You're very good at being unobtrusive while you shoot. Must get you some great candid shots."

"It helps when they're not aware of the camera," Holly agreed, always eager to discuss her work. "People tend to freeze in front of the lens. If I blend with the scenery, I get more natural-looking photos."

"Nice equipment you were using. A Hasselblad camera?"

"Why, yes, it is."

"You're interested in photography, Chance?" Liz asked.

He shrugged slightly. "Used to be," he admitted. "I took some photography classes in high school, shot photos for the school paper and yearbook. It was never anything serious."

What were his hobbies now? Or was he, like her, too wrapped up in his work to make time for outside interests? She was still uncertain whether there was a special woman in his life, and wondered if his kisses the night before had just been a way to pass the time while he was in Atlanta, or part of his campaign to win her over to his side.

"I'll be shooting your brother's wedding," Holly informed Chance blithely. "Sara and Phillip are such a well-matched couple. They'll be a pleasure to work with."

Liz shot a look of exasperation at her outspoken friend, knowing Holly's reference to Phillip's wedding was deliberate—a way of testing Chance's reaction.

Chance only nodded, his eyes turning briefly to Liz. She assumed he knew she'd told Holly the way he felt about the engagement. He obviously aimed not to react to Holly's subtle challenge. "Then perhaps we'll meet again," he said blandly.

Undaunted, Holly nodded and announced that she had to go. She picked up her camera bag from the small table beside them, having already stashed the bulk of her equipment in her minivan. "I've got another wedding to shoot tonight," she said, looking down at her oversize Mickey Mouse watch. "In less than an hour, actually. Bye, Liz. Nice to meet you, Chance. See you at your brother's wedding."

"You're not working the wedding she's going to now?" Chance asked when Holly had dashed off. He'd ignored her parting shot altogether.

Liz shook her head. "I usually recommend Holly's services when I plan a wedding, but she and I don't always work together. I work with several other local photographers and she is often contacted by other consultants or brides making their own arrangements. Sometimes—like today—we work on a subcontract basis. The bride will make out one check to me and I'll issue checks to the florist and musicians, to Holly and the caterers. Other times each vendor bills for his or her own services. It all depends on how much the bride wants me to handle independently."

"And the more you're involved, the more you charge?" Chance speculated.

"That's right. I tailor my services to the wedding budget."

Chance looked thoughtful.

Liz couldn't help laughing at his expression. "You still think it's a waste of money, don't you?" she accused him good-naturedly.

He had the grace to look sheepish. "I still think they'd be smarter to elope and spend all that money on rent and groceries."

"How depressingly practical. Have you no romance in your soul?" Liz teased.

Before she could anticipate his movement, he wrapped a strong arm around her waist and pulled her closer, his mouth hovering only inches above her own. "Why don't you find out for yourself?" he challenged gruffly.

Whatever she might have answered was interrupted by Holly's return. "Whoops," she said, skidding to a halt beside them. "I left my glasses lying on this table. Sorry if I'm interrupting anything."

Her heart racing, Liz pulled quickly out of Chance's arms. "You weren't," she said, hoping her voice sounded more normal to Holly than it did to herself.

"Unfortunately," Chance added plaintively.

Holly giggled as Liz blushed brightly, much to her chagrin. She knew Holly would tease her mercilessly the next time they were alone together. She'd worry about that later. She was more concerned at the moment about being alone again with Chance.

# 5

IT WAS UNSEASONABLY warm for late November—perfect weather for being outdoors. Chance impulsively suggested a fishing trip as he and Liz drove away from the hotel where the wedding reception had been held. Basically he wanted to see Liz in his own kind of setting to remind himself yet again why he shouldn't want her as much as he did. He'd thought watching her at the wedding would drive home how different they were—in their jobs, their education, their interests. It had, of course. And yet, he still wanted her.

"Fishing?" Liz repeated, shocked. "Tomorrow?"

"Yeah. You don't have a Sunday-morning wedding to direct, do you?"

"Well, no. I'm not working tomorrow, but—"

"If you'd rather, we could go white-water rafting on the Chattahoochee. Should still be warm enough—as long as we don't tip over, of course."

Liz glanced away from the road again to glare at Chance. "You think I've never been rafting?"

"You mean you have?" he asked with surprise.

She cleared her throat. "Well, only once, when I was thirteen. I went with a group of Neal's friends without telling my parents. I ended up in the river. Twice. Neal fished me out both times."

Chance grinned. "Did you have fun?"

She laughed. "I had a wonderful time." Her smile faded. "Until I got home. My parents made their displeasure painfully clear. I was grounded for weeks."

"I take it your parents were strict?"

"You could say that," she agreed dryly. "I was hardly allowed to breathe without permission."

"What about Neal? Was he in trouble for taking you along?"

"Neal was twenty-one, living on his own with a two-year-old daughter. He and my parents hadn't had much to do with each other since Sara was born. There was nothing they could do to punish him. They forbade me to have anything to do with him after that. They said he was a bad influence on me," she added with a bitter laugh. "That didn't stop me from seeing him, of course. So I had to lie about being at the library or a friend's house when I visited him and Sara."

Chance waited for her to continue. When she didn't, he asked, "Neal's what—ten years older than you?"

"Eight."

"Almost the same as between Phillip and me," he pointed out, intrigued by the coincidence.

"Yes. I guess that's why I understand the way you feel responsible for him. Neal's always been that way by me."

"Are there any brothers or sisters between you?"

"There was a sister. She died in an accident when she was two, before I was born. I suppose that's one reason my parents were so overly protective of me."

"What happened to make your brother break away from them when Sara was born?" Chance asked, hoping the frank question would receive an equally honest answer.

"That's a long story," Liz said evasively. The wariness between them that had disappeared returned. Probably Liz thought he was seeking information about Neal and Sara to build his case. Two days earlier, he would have been. But now his motives had changed— he wanted to discover all he could about Liz.

"So, how about it?" he asked lightly, hoping to draw her out. "Want to go fishing?"

Liz pulled the car into her assigned space in the parking garage of her apartment building. When she'd killed the engine she faced Chance with a troubled frown. "I don't understand why you're staying in Atlanta, why you're spending so much time with me," she said. "Phillip won't be back until Monday and you said you need to get back to Birmingham. So why are you still here?"

He reached out, pulling her gently close. "You haven't figured that out?"

Her eyes widened. "But, Chance—"

"I know," he muttered, his mouth hovering over hers. "We're on opposite sides of a family conflict, and opposite ends of the society scale, but the fact is, I want

you. And the way you're trembling right now, the way
you're looking at me, makes it seem like it's not one-
sided. Is it, Liz?"

"You know it isn't," she whispered. "But—"

He didn't want to hear the buts. It was enough that
she'd all but admitted she wanted him, too. He lowered his head to hers, losing himself again in her kiss.
As she had before, she hesitated before responding—
but when she did, her response damned near curled his
toes. A mouth shaped for passion, he'd thought the first
time he'd seen her. How right he'd been!

He deepened his kiss, darting his tongue between her
teeth to taste the sweetness inside. He felt her arms slide
around his neck as her tongue touched his in greeting.
He groaned and devoured her mouth with his own.

They were both breathing hard when the kiss ended,
both trembling with the force of their passion. Chance
noted with pleasure that Liz didn't look cool and composed now; just the opposite, in fact—her soft blond
hair mussed, her cheeks flushed, eyes bright. He
groaned as he pictured her in bed, her tangled hair
spread over a pillow, her satiny skin sheened with desire.

"This has nothing to do with Phillip or Sara."

"No," Liz agreed, her voice unusually husky.
"But—"

"So are we on for the fishing trip?" he asked.

"I suppose so," she said. "But— Where will you stay
tonight?"

He looked deeply into her eyes. "I was hoping to stay with you again."

"You were?"

"Yes. Only not on the couch this time," he added daringly, almost holding his breath in anticipation of her reaction.

She paused for what seemed like a very long time, then sighed and gave him a shaky smile. "No," she whispered. "Not on the couch this time."

She'd hardly finished the sentence when his mouth covered hers again.

LIZ WAS SO CONSCIOUS of Chance that, as she put her purse and jacket away, her mind whirled with nerves, doubts and excitement. It was only seven in the evening. Should she start dinner, offer him a drink? Or would he want to go straight to . . .

"Liz." His deep voice was warm with amusement as he stepped close behind her, his big, hard hands falling gently on her shoulders. "Relax. I'm not going to attack you."

She took a deep breath, grateful that he stood behind her so he couldn't see her embarrassment. "I'm sorry. I guess I'm a little nervous. It's been such a long time for me—and we've only known each other a few days—and—um—"

He chuckled and kissed the back of her neck, beneath her neatly upswept hair. "Actually, it's a relief to know I'm not alone in turning into a basket case over this."

"What do you mean?"

"Liz, I've been acting out of character ever since I arrived, Wednesday. Haven't you realized that? I had only planned to stay overnight if Phillip *was* here. I've been calling home, making excuses to Nadine and the job foremen, coming up with all sorts of implausible arguments to stay here. But it all comes down to just one reason—*you*. How many times do I have to tell you this has nothing to do with my brother or his engagement?"

"But we can't just forget about that," Liz reminded him weakly, finding it difficult to stifle the urge to melt against him. "You're still opposed to the engagement, and I still refuse to help you try to end it."

"Look, Phillip and your family won't be back until Monday," Chance pointed out. "I'd rather use the time we have left concentrating on us, on what's happening between us. Let's forget about the others for now, okay?"

"I don't know if we can do that," Liz whispered.

"We can try."

She moistened her lips and nodded. "Yes. We can try."

He smiled. "Now that we have that out of the way..."

Liz tensed, knowing where they were headed.

"What?"

"I'm starving," he said, his eyes gleaming with amusement at her startled reaction. "Think we could rustle up a sandwich or something?"

She smiled. "I suppose we could 'rustle up' a sandwich or something. I may even have a bag of chips to go with it."

"Sounds great." He brushed her mouth lightly with his own. "I like mustard," he said gravely.

"I'll remember that," she assured him, relieved that he'd given her a momentary reprieve. She wanted him; she accepted that now. But the thought of actually making love with him terrified her almost as much as it excited her. Something told her that her safe, orderly life would never be the same afterward.

AT CHANCE'S SUGGESTION, they ate their sandwiches on the living-room floor in front of the television. "Loosen up, Liz," he mocked when she looked startled. "This isn't a formal tea party. It's just sandwiches. Don't you ever eat in front of the tube?"

"Well, no," she admitted, settling gingerly on the floor and arranging her skirt primly over her legs. "I've always been in the habit of eating at a table."

"Even when you eat alone?"

"Yes, of course."

He sighed deeply. "You probably even set the table formally for you. Salad fork, linen napkin, water goblet. Am I right?"

She cleared her throat, uncomfortable with his teasing. "Well . . ."

"I thought so. Has anyone ever told you that you tend to be a bit compulsive, Liz?"

"Yes," she replied with a sigh. "Several people have mentioned that, as a matter of fact. I can't help it. I guess I'm just made that way."

Sitting cross-legged on her plush carpet, his plate on one knee, a canned soda beside him, Chance reached out to pat her hand consolingly. "Don't sweat it," he said. "All you need is a little practice at being spontaneous."

She tilted her head quizzically, determined not to let him best her. "Can one really practice being spontaneous?" she asked.

He grinned. "One can only try."

She laughed and shook her head. "Eat your sandwiches, Chance."

Chance flipped channels with the remote control until he found an old Patrick Swayze and Sam Elliott movie on cable. He watched it as he ate the two oversize sandwiches Liz had put together for him. Liz watched for a while, but even Swayze's frequently bared chest couldn't make the gory violence appealing to her. Instead, she observed Chance.

His strong profile was even more appealing to her now than that first time she'd seen him, when he'd affected her so unexpectedly, so deeply. Muscles rippled in his arms and back when he reached for his soda; his corded throat worked as he tilted his head back to swallow his drink. She shivered with sensual awareness when his eyes met hers over the soda can.

At that point, Chance lost interest in the movie, turning his full concentration on Liz. He set his soda can on the empty plate beside him, never looking away from her. "God, you're beautiful."

Suddenly flustered—as shy as a schoolgirl, she thought reproachfully—she reached for his plate and stacked it with her own. "I'll just go put these away," she murmured, regretting her light complexion, which must now be blushing a deep pink.

Chance didn't answer, but the television set went silent as she walked into the kitchen. Her throat tightened.

He was standing in the doorway when she turned from loading the dishwasher. "Are you afraid of me, Liz?" he asked with concern.

"No," she answered honestly. "I'm afraid of the way you make me feel."

His eyebrow lifted inquiringly. "Why?"

She twisted her hands in front of her. "What if we're making a mistake? What if we're allowing ourselves to be carried away by attraction now, only to regret it later?"

"Then we'll deal with it as it comes," he replied evenly. "We're not kids, Liz. We know what we're doing."

"What *are* we doing?" she asked in little more than a whisper. "What are we starting?"

He took a step closer to her. "Do you always have to analyze everything, put labels on your feelings?"

"Yes," she said simply. "Always."

His smile was spine-melting. "Then it's time for a change. You're supposed to be practicing spontaneity, remember?"

Her own smile felt decidedly tremulous. "Yes. I remember."

He held out his hand to her. "Come here and be spontaneous with me."

Taking a deep breath, Liz stepped forward and placed her hand in his.

Chance pulled her into his arms. "I have wanted you from the first moment I saw you," he murmured, his voice oddly hoarse. "Even when I assumed you'd never look twice at someone like me."

"Someone like you?" she repeated, confused by his wording.

He nodded. "Rough around the edges," he explained. "Blue-collar all the way to my boots."

Did it really bother him so much that he was the son of a plumber and she the daughter of an old-money family? He didn't give her an opportunity to assure him that neither his background nor his occupation could lessen her feelings for him. Instead, he covered her mouth with his own, passionately sweeping her away.

She couldn't speak when he kissed her like this; could hardly think coherently. No other man had ever shattered her composure so utterly with nothing more than his kisses. She couldn't envision what his lovemaking would do to her—but was shockingly eager to find out.

Sliding her arms around his neck, she rose on tiptoe to deepen the kiss, pressing herself close to Chance for the first time. His lean, fit body felt as good against her as she'd imagined it would—strong, solid, hard. He made her feel utterly feminine, infinitely desirable. It was a heady, strangely liberating feeling.

As if in a trance, she led him to her bedroom, where her passion built under the impact of his deep, rapacious kisses. Her hesitancy gone, her doubts shoved ruthlessly to the back of her mind, she participated eagerly, feverishly, tugging at his clothing as he skillfully dispensed with hers.

Naked, they clung together beside the bed, sharing the seductive pleasure of warm, bare skin, rapid pulses, ragged breathing. Liz closed her eyes and savored the crisp brush of the hair on his chest and legs, the hot, pulsing of his erection pressing into her abdomen. It had been so long, she realized dreamily, holding him more tightly—so very long since she'd allowed herself to want someone this way, to unleash the tightly reined sensual side of her nature.

Chance began a slow, painstaking exploration of her body, beginning at the hollow of her throat, moving leisurely down to her breasts and stomach. Her hands clenched at his shoulders. When he moved lower still, she gasped.

"Chance," she whispered, her body tense. Were they making a mistake? Would they regret this when the night was over?

As if sensing her fears, Chance murmured unintelligible reassurances, his hands stroking gently, his kisses deepening, lingering. She shuddered, but this time from arousal rather than fear. "Oh, Chance!"

Chance lowered her gently to the bed, his mouth locked to hers as he followed. He gave her no further opportunity for doubts or inhibitions, his silent, forceful lovemaking driving her further and further into the hot, mindless grip of passion. He made love the way he did everything else, she thought dazedly, holding tightly to his sweat-slick shoulders. With single-minded concentration. She knew he was thinking of nothing or no one but her, just as he gave her no time to think of anything but him, of the emotions he roused in her, of the ability she seemed to have to evoke equally powerful responses from him.

She cried out when her climax rocked her. He groaned her name only moments later, his body arching deeply into hers. Then they collapsed into the sheets, panting, shuddering, clinging to the last ripples of pleasure. Chance buried his face in her throat. Liz stroked his hair while her pulse slowed and her eyes focused blindly on the ceiling.

She'd worried earlier that nothing would ever be the same if she and Chance made love. And she'd been right—because now she knew without a doubt that her life had changed irrevocably.

She was also falling in love with the man who held the power to ruin her beloved niece's life. For the life of her, Liz didn't know how she could face choosing between her loyalty to Sara and her overwhelming feelings for Chance.

# 6

THE BEDROOM WAS pitch-dark when Chance gently shook Liz awake. Grumbling a protest, she burrowed deeper into the pillow, only to be shaken more forcefully. "Time to get up, Liz," he said cheerfully.

"You must be joking," she muttered, opening one eye just long enough to focus in horror on the bedside clock. Chance snapped on the lamp, flooding the room with painful light.

"Got to get out on the lake early to catch fish," he assured her. "Rise and shine, sweetheart."

She groaned, unable to believe anyone could be so cheerful after so little sleep. Had she known he'd planned to get up before dawn, she might have insisted they go to sleep an hour sooner. *Well, maybe not.* She smiled dreamily into the pillow.

It hadn't taken Chance long to distract her from her uneasiness following their initial lovemaking. He'd kept her thoroughly diverted until they'd both fallen into exhausted sleep in the middle of the night. How could he possibly be so full of energy now when she felt as though she'd hardly slept at all?

She heard him rummaging in her walk-in closet. "Haven't you got any jeans that don't have designer labels on the pockets?" he complained loudly enough for her to hear. "What do you clean house in, business suits?"

"I don't clean house," she replied, rolling onto her back with a resigned sigh. "I hire someone for that."

"Of course, you do." He reappeared at the side of the bed and tossed a pullover and jeans at her. "These should work. You've got ten minutes to get dressed or I'll stuff you into them myself."

"Have I mentioned that I don't like bossy males?" Liz asked with a scowl, and reaching for her robe, she reluctantly sat up.

"A time or two," he replied, amused. "But I *did* ask you if you wanted to go fishing with me this morning. Remember?"

"And I said yes." She sighed.

"You said yes. So up and at 'em, Liz. We're burning daylight."

"*What* daylight?" she grumbled, not expecting an answer.

It took a little more than ten minutes for Liz to put on the jeans and pink fleece pullover Chance had selected for her, but he didn't complain. He prepared a quick breakfast while she dressed and applied a minimum of makeup—she wouldn't even face *fish* without her mascara. She brushed her hair, then tied it into a ponytail to keep it out of the way.

"Just what are we supposed to fish with, anyway?" she demanded, when she reached the kitchen, gratefully accepting the cup of coffee Chance held out to her. "I don't even own a rod."

"No problem. I carry a couple of rods and a tackle box in the back of my pickup."

She lifted an eyebrow in question. "Always?"

He grinned. "Always. Never know when I'll be hit with the urge to fish."

She'd wondered if he had any hobbies. It seemed he did. "Does that urge hit you often?"

He shrugged. "I'm lucky if I get to go once a month. The business keeps me pretty busy."

"Now that sounds familiar," she said with a smile, scooping a blueberry out of the cereal Chance had poured for her. Two slices of toast, dripping with butter and jam, sat on a plate beside her, along with a small glass of orange juice and a cup of coffee.

"So, what do you do for fun?" Chance asked, rapidly dispensing with his own breakfast. "All you've done since I've been here is work."

"Like you, my business takes up most of my time. But I enjoy going to movies and theater productions with friends. Holly and Devon and I get together at least once a month for dinner and a show."

"Devon?"

"Oh, that's right, you haven't met her. She's a dress designer, specializing in wedding gowns. She and I have been friends for several years, and when we met Holly two years ago, we became a close threesome. We're all single and in the same business, so we have a great deal in common."

"You don't have any favorite sports?" Chance seemed to find it hard to believe that dinner and a theater production were her idea of a good time. She could almost picture him engaged in some strenuous physical activity—volleyball, maybe—stripped to the waist, muscles rippling as he spiked a ball over a net, his tanned skin filmed with sweat, his dark hair plastered to his head. She shivered in immediate reaction to the arousing image.

"Liz?" he prodded.

She cleared her throat loudly, relieved that he couldn't read her mind. "No, I really don't participate in any sports, other than an occasional tennis match with Neal or Sara," she admitted. "I try to stay in shape by taking an occasional aerobic dance class at a local health club, but it's hard to make time for it. When I was younger, I wanted—" She broke off with a self-conscious laugh. "Well, never mind that."

She should have known he wouldn't let her get away with the evasion. "What did you want?" he demanded.

"I wanted to join a softball team," she confessed shyly. "For some reason, I thought that would be a lot of fun. My parents wouldn't let me, of course. They were older than most parents of girls my age, and very old-fashioned and straitlaced in some ways. According to them, softball wasn't a feminine pursuit, so they

enrolled me in piano classes. I enjoy playing sometimes, though I'd never be able to make my living as a
concert pianist."

"So how come you haven't remarried?" Chance
asked, suddenly changing the subject.

"I haven't been in any hurry to remarry," she said,
reaching for her juice to avoid looking at him. "It wasn't
an experience I remember fondly."

"Did he mistreat you?" An edge of belligerence
sharpened Chance's deep voice.

"Not physically," Liz assured him. "But Jim was a
man who had to control everything and everyone
around him, including his wife. After we were married, he became obsessed with maintaining his control
over our schedules, our finances, our relationships with
others. He found it very frustrating that he couldn't also
control my thoughts and feelings, though he certainly
tried to do even that. I suppose he's a very insecure
man. I just didn't have the patience or the inclination
to help him overcome those insecurities. By the time
our marriage ended, the only thing I felt for him was
resentment."

"You don't really think I'm like him, do you?" Chance
asked, scowling.

She paused, taking care in phrasing. "I think you're
very accustomed to being in charge, being responsible
for the welfare of others—your stepmother, your
brother, your employees. I think it would be very easy
for you to use that history of responsibility as an ex-

cuse to try to maintain control even when you should step back and allow others to make their own choices."

His frown deepened. "You're talking about Phillip again."

"Of course."

"Liz, I—" He stopped and shook his head. "Never mind. We said we weren't going to talk about my brother today. Let's keep it at that."

"Fine with me," she answered. "But we *will* have to face it again sometime, Chance. They'll be home tomorrow."

"Yeah. Well, today we're going fishing," he said, gathering up their empty plates. "And it's time to go. You ready?"

She quickly drained the last of her coffee. "Yes, I'm ready."

"Good. I'll stack these things in the dishwasher while you grab a jacket. It'll probably be cool on the lake this morning."

She hurried to her bedroom to fetch a jacket. Had their breakfast discussion accomplished anything? She hoped it had at least given Chance a hint that she wouldn't sit meekly back and let him run her life the way he was trying to run his brother's.

Maybe her warning hadn't even been necessary. After all, Chance said nothing about wanting their affair to last beyond this weekend—a prospect she found disturbing and depressing.

THERE WERE A COUPLE of other women at the battered little marina where Chance purchased bait and rented a fishing boat. Still, the atmosphere was very male. Relaxed-looking men in flannel and denim exchanged greetings with Chance as if he were an old friend, while giving Liz only polite nods when they passed. The smell of fish, strong coffee and the exhaust of boat motors hung heavily in the crisp, cool air, but it was an oddly pleasant combination.

Sleepy-eyed, Liz watched Chance select a boat, motor, life jackets and bait. He seemed very much at home in these surroundings. It was the first time since she'd met him that he really seemed comfortable. Had he felt so terribly out of place in her business, working with her at the wedding the day before? As bewilderingly out of his element then as she felt now?

The marina rocked gently beneath her sneakered feet, accompanied by the rhythmic slap of water against the pontoons keeping the faded frame building afloat. Outboard motors sputtered to life, accelerating noisily, then fading away as the fishermen sped off in hopes of a big catch. Not particularly enthused about the prospect of hooking one herself, Liz hoped that Chance wouldn't mind if she curled up in the boat for a nap while he fished.

Lost in thought, she didn't realize at first that Chance was speaking to her, and that both he and the man behind the marina counter were looking at her. Flushing a little at the attention, she asked, "What did you say?"

"I need your birthday, your height and your weight," he repeated. "I managed hair and eye color on my own."

She tilted her head. "Why do you need to know these things?"

"For your fishing license," he explained. "You have to have one to fish legally."

She gave the date and year of her birth and added that she was five feet, seven inches tall.

"Weight?" Chance asked, taking the opportunity to lingeringly admire her figure.

Feeling her flush deepen, Liz gave him a quick glare of reproach before looking at the amused man behind the counter. "One hundred twenty pounds," she muttered.

"That much?" Chance teased, earning himself a punch on the arm. "I was only kidding, Liz," he said soothingly, rubbing the spot where she'd hit him. "You've got a great body. Wouldn't you say so, Joe?" he asked the other man, who grinned.

Gritting her teeth, Liz vowed to dump Chance into the lake. If only she knew how to run an outboard motor, she'd leave him out there!

Laughing, Chance slipped an arm around her waist. "Come on, honey. Let's go catch some fish. The morning's half-gone."

She didn't bother to point out that the sun was barely up, casting a hazy pink glow over the lake. Nor that normally she'd be asleep at this time—even on weekdays. Sighing, she trailed him to the flat-bottomed aluminum boat he'd rented for the morning. His strong, callused hand steadied her as she stepped into the rocking boat.

The bench seat was uncushioned and the metal felt cold even through her jeans. Freezing, Liz huddled into her life jacket as Chance turned the bow toward open water, competently handling the outboard motor. The wind chilled her right through as they headed across the lake. She held on to the sides with numb fingers. They occasionally hit the waves with teeth-jarring thuds. Wiping cold spray from her cheek, Liz glanced over her shoulder at Chance. He looked smugly content. So this was his idea of fun.

Intercepting Liz's glance, Chance smiled. He thought she looked great with loose strands of blond hair whipping around her wind-reddened cheeks, a few hairs clinging to her lips. He dropped his gaze, reminding himself to concentrate on steering the boat. If he allowed himself to dwell on last night, he was quite likely to run into one of the tree stumps poking out of the water. Not that he'd ever be able to forget last night. How could he, when nothing in his life had ever quite compared to those hours in Liz Archer's arms?

He had been pleasantly surprised at how cooperative she'd been so far this morning, though it was obvious she'd never been fishing and would probably have preferred to spend the morning in bed. He'd been equally tempted to do so, and wasn't sure why it had seemed so important to see Liz in his world, rather than her own. He'd assumed that maybe he'd overcome his fascination with her when he saw her awkwardly struggling to adapt. Instead, his interest in her was growing with every minute they spent together.

Whether she caught a fish or not, and regardless of her feelings about the sport, he wanted her. He didn't quite understand it, but he'd fallen hard and fast for this woman. And he didn't for the life of him know what he was going to do about it.

"CHANCE, I REALLY THINK you should let me put some antiseptic and a bandage on your neck. What if it gets infected?"

Chance gingerly rubbed the swollen, angry-looking scratch at the back of his neck. "I'll tell everyone I was bitten by a vampire with dirty teeth."

Liz frowned at him, shepherding him through her apartment toward the bathroom. "Very funny. I insist you let me take care of that for you. After all, I was the one who wounded you."

He snickered.

Liz glared at him. "Don't start laughing again. You certainly didn't think it was funny at the time."

"Yeah, well I had a fishhook sticking out of my neck at the time. I was a little concerned about my jugular."

She pushed him down on the closed lid of the toilet, turning to rummage in the medicine cabinet for antiseptic and a bandage. "It wasn't in your neck, it was in your shirt collar. And you were the one who insisted I had to learn to cast."

"I also told you to watch out where you swung the hook."

"I'd have gotten it out of your shirt without hurting you if you hadn't jerked when you did."

"I had a strike!" he protested. "Biggest damned crappie I've hooked in months!"

"Now you're going to blame me because it got away, right?"

"Well, if you hadn't shrieked just as I was taking it off the hook . . ."

"I did *not* shriek. I simply informed you that I couldn't get the hook out of your collar if you wouldn't be still."

"And then you proceeded to stab me with the sucker, causing me to drop that big crappie right back into the damned lake."

"I wouldn't have stabbed you if you'd been still," she reminded him, swabbing the scabbed-over scratch with an antiseptic-soaked cotton ball.

Chance flinched. "Ouch!"

"Well, that's an improvement over what you said when I accidentally scratched you with the fishhook," she said cheerfully, slapping a bandage over the injury.

"Why is it that you seem to enjoy causing me pain? You're not one of those kinky types, are you? No leather corsets hidden in your underwear drawer?"

She refused to let him get to her with his teasing. "You're just mad because I caught the biggest fish, after all."

"Only because you made me lose mine," he reminded her. "And stop gloating. Who had to clean your fish?"

"From the start, I told you that I would fish with you, I'd even bait my own hook, but I would *not* clean anything we caught," she reminded him in turn.

"You wouldn't even watch."

She shuddered. "No kidding."

He looped his arms around her waist and pulled her between his spread knees. "You will help me cook them, I hope?"

"I'll even help you eat them," she assured him with a smile, resting her forearms on his shoulders.

"Yeah, somehow I thought you'd do that." Tightening his arms around her waist, Chance laid his head on her breasts, closing his eyes contentedly. "I had fun, Liz."

She pressed her cheek to his hair. "So did I," she murmured, holding him close. She was being totally honest—she *had* enjoyed the morning immensely. Chance was wonderful company, amusing and amazingly patient, even when she'd made utterly stupid mistakes. He hadn't even yelled at her when she'd caused him to drop the fish; only given her a disgusted look that had sent her into peals of laughter. Though she'd never been fishing with Jim, who was more the golf-and-racquetball type, she could only imagine how furious he would have been at her clumsiness.

It had been quite a while since she'd laughed with a man the way she'd laughed with Chance that day. Yet, beneath the laughter, the sexual tension between them lingered. And Liz was still plagued by the realization that unfinished business lay ahead of them; that Chance was only passing time with her until his brother returned from Florida. What would happen then?

Liz had no doubt that Phillip would refuse to give in to Chance's demands for him to cancel or postpone the wedding. Phillip was too deeply in love with Sara to be swayed by his brother's pleas. Would Chance then leave in a rage, returning to his life in Birmingham without a backward glance at the family that had taken his brother away from him? Would he blame Liz for refusing to take his side? Would he regret staying with her, making love with someone he might soon consider one of the enemy? Would she ever hear from him after he left?

As if sensing her growing uneasiness, Chance lifted his head to look up at her. "Liz? What's wrong?"

She managed a smile. "Nothing. How's your injury? Better?"

He nuzzled into her neck. "I think it needs a great deal of Liz Archer's own special brand of TLC."

She shivered when his teeth nipped delicately at the vulnerable hollow of her throat. "I thought we were going to cook fish."

"Later." He rose to his feet, sweeping her into his arms as he did so. "Maybe much later."

"Much, much later," she agreed, closing her eyes in pleasure as he moved surely toward the bed.

IT WAS CLOSE TO midnight when they returned to bed, pleasantly full of fried fish, coleslaw and hush puppies. Pulling Liz closer to his chest, Chance snuggled spoon-fashion against her back, one arm beneath her, the other hand resting just below her breasts. "It's been a long day," he murmured. "Tired?"

"Mmm."

"Was that a yes?"

"Yes."

He smiled and held her more tightly, pressing his cheek against her hair. He could get used to sleeping with this woman, he thought drowsily. He usually didn't mind sleeping alone—actually preferred it most of the time—but he suspected that sleeping with Liz in his arms could well prove addictive. Which should have made him nervous, but somehow didn't. "Liz?"

"Mmm?"

"Did you really have a good time today?"

"Yes. I'm not saying I'd want to go fishing every weekend, but today was fun."

"So, how do you feel about hiking and camping?"

She groaned. "Right now I wouldn't even have the energy to hike to the bathroom."

"I wasn't talking about right now. I meant—maybe some other time."

He felt her contented drowsiness dissipate. "You mean, like sometime in the future?" she asked carefully.

"Yeah. Sometime in the future. What do you think?"

She was quiet for several long moments, and then said, very softly, "I think we'd better talk about this again later."

It wasn't hard to guess what concerned her about making plans for their future. "After Phillip and your family return from Florida, you mean."

"Yes."

"You can't accept that whatever we have together has nothing to do with them, can you?"

"I know it doesn't now," she replied, lying very still in his arms. "But I'm afraid it will make a big difference later. Especially if you can never learn to accept Phillip and Sara's engagement—or their marriage."

"You think this is going to drive a permanent wedge between Phillip and me, don't you? That Phillip and Sara will refuse to have anything more to do with me—and vice versa—and that you'll be stuck in the middle."

"Not exactly."

He frowned at the correction. "No. You won't be in the middle. You'll be on their side, won't you?"

She squirmed restlessly. "I didn't say that."

"You didn't have to."

She looked over her shoulder, straining to see him in the darkness. "Don't make me choose, Chance. Please. You may insist on forcing a choice on your brother, but I don't want you to do that to me."

He sighed deeply and shook his head. "You seem obstinate about refusing to see my side. You act as though I'm hoping for a fight, for a major crisis. I'm not, you know. I hope to settle everything peacefully. I'm not going to ask Phillip to stop seeing Sara. I only hope to convince him that he's being foolish and impulsive to throw aside years of planning for an impetuous decision made in the heat of his first real love."

"Put it to him like that and you'll have a major crisis on your hands whether you're hoping for one or not," Liz warned darkly. "Honestly, Chance, can't you hear how arrogant you sound? How pompous? Phillip knows what he's doing, what he wants. He's in love, but he's not an infatuated fool being led by the nose into a catastrophe. He may have proposed to Sara on impulse, but they've talked a lot about what they're doing and believe it's the right move for them. Who are you to say it's not?"

"We keep coming back to the same arguments, don't we?"

"Yes."

For Chance, this ill-advised love affair of Phillip's was growing into an overwhelming problem. First it had made Phillip withdraw from his family to the extent that he'd announced his engagement in a letter—a damned impersonal letter—and canceled his longtime plans to join Cassidy Construction. Now it had become a wedge between himself and the most fascinating, exciting woman he'd met in years.

Sure, he and Liz had a few problems that had nothing to do with their respective families. Despite her good-natured acceptance of the fishing excursion, Chance still suspected she was a bit too blue-blooded for him, too champagne-and-caviar to his hot-dogs-and-beer. And, of course, she owned a business in Atlanta and he was firmly rooted in Birmingham; he wasn't sure a long-distance romance would last very long, anyway. But, damn, he wanted her—as much or more, now that he'd made love with her, than when he'd first met her.

So, where did that leave them?

"Maybe we'd just better drop it for now and get some sleep," he said wearily, refusing to let anything else come between them tonight. She felt too good in his arms for him to release her now.

"Ignoring it won't make it go away," Liz reminded him wistfully.

"I know. But talking about it now won't do any good, either."

"No," she agreed with a sigh, relaxing against him. "Good night, Chance."

"Night, honey."

But it was a long time before he slept. And he was awake again before dawn, his undiminished hunger for

Liz overcoming his consideration for her rest. She didn't protest when he turned her in his arms to wake her with a kiss. Instead, her arms wrapped around him as if she'd been waiting for him to awaken, as eager as he to experience their uniquely special lovemaking again. Neither of them was disappointed. Their mingled cries of satisfaction echoed softly through her quiet apartment.

The next time Chance awoke, full sunlight was streaming through the curtains of Liz's bedroom. He was alone in the bed. Shoving a hand through his disheveled hair, he sat up, suddenly realizing that he was alone in the apartment. Liz had left for work. The weekend was over.

He wondered what the day ahead held for them. Whether whatever they'd found would survive. And he couldn't help wondering whether it mattered as much to Liz as it did to him.

# 7

SHE'D MADE A MISTAKE getting involved with Chance. A potentially devastating mistake, Liz thought morosely, staring blindly at one wall of her office on Monday. She was having a very difficult time concentrating on work, her thoughts turning all too frequently to the man she'd left sleeping in her bed that morning.

Their late-night conversation kept reverberating in her mind. Chance had expressed interest in seeing her again, even after this weekend, yet he'd refused to reconsider his decision to attempt to talk Phillip out of his wedding and career plans. Liz was convinced that the confrontation would end bitterly. Battle lines would be drawn, and Liz and Chance would find themselves on opposite sides, as he'd predicted last night. How could they not? She was adamant about helping Sara and Phillip plan the wedding. Surely Chance would resent her participation.

She dreaded the afternoon. Family conflicts were always distressing to her, probably because she'd seen so many of them between her parents and her brother. She couldn't bear to think of Sara being hurt by Chance's rejection of her before he'd even met her. But, most of all, Liz couldn't bear to consider the possibility of a rift between Chance and herself. Now that she'd been with him, laughed with him, made love with him, how could she ever go back to being strangers with him?

She never should have allowed herself to get involved with him. Her sigh echoed in the quiet office.

A tap on the door proved a welcome distraction. "Liz? Got a minute?"

Liz looked up with a smile. "Hi, Devon. What's up?"

Looking even more slender and fragile than usual in an oversize sweater and double-pleated wool slacks, Devon stepped into the office, carrying a large sketchbook. "I passed Marcy as she left for lunch and she said you were between appointments—but if you're busy, I can drop by later."

"I'm never too busy to see you," Liz answered. "Want a cup of tea?"

Devon shook her head. "No, thanks. I was in the neighborhood and thought I'd stop by with the preliminary sketches for Rhonda MacLaughlin's wedding gown. I'd like your opinion before I show it to her, since you know how worried she is about finding a gown that suits her figure."

"I'd love to see it. But I assured her when I recommended you that I was confident you'd be able to design a beautiful gown for her, that you've had experience designing for larger women."

Devon grimaced. "She's so sensitive about her appearance. She's convinced that only brides with tiny waists and long, thin legs look beautiful on their wedding day, despite the photographs I've shown her to the contrary. She really needs to work on that inferiority complex of hers."

Reaching for the sketch pad, Liz nodded. "Maybe Chuck can help her with that problem. He's so obviously crazy about her. I've heard him tell her more than once that he finds her beautiful and that he can't wait to see her coming down the aisle in her Devon Fleming gown. I don't know how she can hold on to that inferiority complex now that she's found someone who thinks she's darned near perfect."

"I hope you're right. So, what do you think?"

Liz examined the sketches with pleased approval. "Devon, you're a genius. I don't know how you do it, but this design is absolutely wonderful. Rhonda's going to adore it."

"You really think so? I like it, but I wasn't sure—after all, you know Rhonda better than I do."

"Trust me. It's great. You've even made the woman in the sketches look just like her, so she'll have a clear idea of how the dress will look on her. Very clever, Dev."

Characteristically, Devon flushed rosily at the compliment. Despite the fact that she'd made quite a name for herself as a designer, had even been courted by two large, prestigious retailers to add her lines to their inventory, Devon was uncomfortable with the praise and attention she received for her work. Basically shy and introverted, nonetheless Devon had come a long way during the years Liz had known her.

Devon was also unusually perceptive. She and Liz had only been talking for a few minutes when Devon closed her sketchbook and leaned forward, studying Liz's face with concern. "What's wrong, Liz?"

"I—uh— What do you mean?"

"Something's really bothering you. Do you want to talk about it? Does it have anything to do with Phillip's brother being in town? Holly told me about it," she added in response to Liz's unspoken question.

Liz sighed and nodded. "It has *everything* to do with Chance being in town."

"You're upset because he's opposed to Sara's engagement to Phillip? Do you think there's a chance he'll succeed in breaking them up?"

"No," Liz answered emphatically. "Knowing Sara and Phillip, I don't think anyone could break them up. But it's entirely possible that the Cassidy family could be split over Chance's disapproval. I think Phillip made his choice clear when he mailed the letter to his mother and brother announcing the engagement. I think he was saying then that he knew Chance wouldn't approve, but he was willing to sacrifice his relationship with his brother in favor of his love for Sara. I'm sure it will tear Phillip apart. I believe he's been close to his family until now. But I can't see him changing his mind about marrying Sara."

"Holly said you'd tried to warn Chance, but he wouldn't believe you."

"He believes Phillip will 'listen to reason,' as he puts it."

Devon's lips curled in distaste. "Is he really as stuffy and arrogant as that sounds?"

A few days earlier, Liz might have said yes. But that was before she'd spent time with Chance, before she'd made love with him. "I don't think so," she said. "Not really. It's just with Phillip. He's been so accustomed to guiding Phillip's life, to playing the role of wiser older brother and surrogate father, that he can't accept that it's time to back off and allow Phillip to choose his own way."

"Knowing the way you feel about people who try to control others, I'm surprised you're being so tolerant of him," Devon commented. Devon knew all about Liz's experiences with her parents and ex-husband.

"Well, he's—really very nice in some ways."

"You know, I thought Holly was exaggerating about your personal interest in Phillip's brother, but I may have been wrong. Was I?"

"He's— We've— I—" Liz was frustrated by her inability to verbalize her feelings for Chance, as much as she would have liked to talk to Devon about her vulnerability and confusion. "Oh, Devon, I'm really in a mess this time," she said.

"Do you want to tell me about it?" Devon repeated, always careful not to overstep the bounds of friendship in unwelcome prying.

"I wish I could," Liz answered wearily. "Maybe it's all too new, too overwhelming just now. I've fallen for him, Devon. Fallen hard. But I can't see anything but heartache coming from it. Even if we weren't so different, even if we didn't live so far apart, even if he didn't remind me too much of Jim in some ways, this thing with Sara and Phillip would still come between us. All together, it's just too much to handle."

"Oh, Liz, I'm sorry. Is there anything I can do?"

Liz tried to smile and shook her head. "No. Not now, anyway. Though maybe you'll be around sometime when I need to talk, when I need a sympathetic shoulder?"

"Always," Devon promised without hesitation.

"Thanks, Dev. That means a lot to me."

"I know you'd do the same for me," Devon replied.

"Of course, I would."

"Have you—?"

Whatever question Devon had intended to ask was interrupted by a sharp double rap on the door. Without waiting for a response, Chance poked his head around the door. "Liz? Oh, sorry, I didn't know you were with anyone. There's no one out here at the desk and . . ."

Liz stood. "No, it's all right, Chance. Come on in, I want you to meet someone."

She was relieved to see that he was smiling when he entered. He looked so much less intimidating when he smiled—and Devon was easily intimidated. "Devon Fleming, this is Chance Cassidy."

"Mr. Cassidy," Devon murmured, coolly.

Liz wasn't really surprised by Devon's behavior. Fiercely loyal, notoriously softhearted, close to both Liz and Sara, Devon would naturally feel antagonistic toward anyone who threatened their happiness.

Chance's eyes narrowed a bit at the unencouraging greeting, but he managed to maintain his smile. "It's nice to meet you. And, please, call me Chance."

"Your brother looks quite a bit like you. I would have known immediately that you're related to Phillip."

"We've been told we take after our father," Chance agreed, glancing searchingly at Liz, as if waiting for her to rescue him from the awkward situation.

"Phillip and Sara make a very attractive couple. I'm to design her gown, you know. She'll be a beautiful bride."

"Liz tells me that you're a very talented designer," Chance responded noncommittally.

"Liz is very loyal to her friends—and loved ones," Devon replied.

Wincing a bit at Devon's brittle tone, Liz quickly interceded. "What brings you here, Chance? Was there something you needed?"

"I was hoping I'd catch you in time to take you out to lunch. Do you have any other plans?"

"No. That sounds nice, thank you."

Chance turned to Devon, courtesy prompting him to say, "Would you join us, Devon? I'd enjoy the chance to get to know you better, since you and Liz are so close."

"Thank you, but no. I have other plans." Tucking her sketchbook into the crook of her arm, Devon turned to Liz, her brown eyes warming immediately. "I'll talk to you later, okay, Liz? Call me."

"I will. And I love the gown, Devon. I know Rhonda will be pleased."

"Hope you're right. Goodbye, Mr. Cassidy."

The office door closed behind Devon. Immediately, Chance confronted Liz. "Why is it that your friends behave as if they're meeting a slimy criminal when you introduce me?" he demanded.

"Holly and Devon are very fond of Sara," Liz answered simply. "They're afraid you're going to hurt her."

"Maybe they're concerned about their fees if the wedding's canceled," he suggested.

"That's ridiculous," Liz replied indignantly, incensed by his accusation. "One wedding, more or less, will hardly matter to either of them, since they both have all the business they can handle now. Besides, neither Holly nor Devon will make a profit on her wedding, given the fact they're going to discount their services."

"Dammit, can't we spend even five minutes together without coming back to this?" Chance asked irritably.

"Apparently not. Do you still want to have lunch?"

"Don't you need to lock up or something?"

"Yes. I'll just be a minute."

"Take your time. I'm in no hurry." He shoved his hands into the pockets of his leather jacket as if prepared to wait all day for her.

Liz hurried anyway, hoping that she and Chance would be able to have lunch together without arguing.

Somehow they managed it, but only by very carefully avoiding any mention of Sara and Phillip. Both were acutely aware that they had only a few hours to ignore their main source of conflict.

TOO TENSE AND WORRIED all afternoon to concentrate on her work, Liz left the office an hour earlier than usual, grateful that she'd scheduled no late appointments that day. She drove straight home, wondering if Chance would be there, whether Neal, Sara and Phillip had gotten back in town yet, whether Chance and Phillip had already argued. She hadn't heard from any of them during the interminable hours since lunch.

As she'd loaned Chance a key to her place, she wasn't surprised to find him sitting on her couch, reading one of her books. "Hi," she said, pausing just inside the door to smile tentatively at him.

Chance set the book aside. "You're home early, aren't you?"

"A bit. Slow afternoon," she explained vaguely. "Have you been here since lunch?"

He nodded and rose to his feet. "I wasn't in the mood for sight-seeing," he replied, taking a step toward her.

"Oh?" She wet her lips, noting the smoldering look in his darkened eyes. "What—um— What *are* you in the mood for?"

Taking her purse out of her hands, he tossed it aside. "Guess."

She reached for him even as his hands closed around her waist and his mouth came down hard on hers.

Liz closed her eyes and wrapped her arms around his neck, realizing that she had hoped he'd be waiting for her when she came home early, hoped they'd have at least one more chance to be together. If the worst occurred, at least she'd have one more special memory of Chance to savor when he was gone.

His tongue plunged into her mouth, hungry and urgent. She tilted her head to deepen the kiss, her own tongue welcoming, tangling eagerly with his. He hadn't kissed her even once at lunch. She'd known then that he'd been concerned that he wouldn't be able to stop at that if he did. The passion between them was too strong to be assuaged with kisses.

Suddenly, smoothly, he lifted her, taking a step forward to pin her to the door, his strong body pressing into her. He kissed her again and again, deeply, ravishingly, but still it wasn't enough—for either of them.

She threaded her fingers into his hair, kicked off her shoes and wrapped her legs around his lean, denim-covered hips, the full skirt of her floral cotton dress offering no resistance to her movements. Chance was already erect. He pressed his hips against her. Her legs tightened.

"Chance," she whispered brokenly. "Oh, Chance, I want you so much."

Her words seemed to arouse him even more. He groaned and buried his face in her throat, his lips moving just above the scoop neckline of the dress. "Liz," he muttered. "I want— I can't—"

Still holding her pressed to the door, he reached beneath her skirt, his large, callused hands on her thighs sending heat through her thin stockings. She tangled her fingers in the hair at the back of his head and tugged, lifting his face back to hers. His breath was warm against her skin when she ran her lips along his jaw, stroked the tip of her tongue across his lower lip, then kissed the shallow indentation in his chin.

He pushed at her legs, urging her to stand. She did so, expecting to be led immediately to the bedroom. Instead, he reached again beneath her skirt and swiftly removed her panty hose and panties. Without hesitating, she stepped out of them, startled but intrigued. Was he going to take her right here?

It seemed he was. His mouth on hers, he lifted her against the door again, arranging her legs back around him. He fumbled a moment with the front of his jeans and then he was against her, hot, swollen, throbbing. Her breath lodged in her throat, preventing any sound but one tight gasp from escaping her lips.

One sure, sinuous thrust took him deep inside her. Shuddering, she clung to him, her cheek pressed to his hair, her ankles locked behind his back. It crossed her mind that someone passing her apartment in the outer hallway might wonder at the soft thump-thump-thump coming from her door, but what did she care?

With one arm steadying her, Chance slid his other hand between them and did something with his fingertips that made her jerk against him as though jolted with electricity. "Chance!"

He kissed her and moved his fingers again. An explosion of sensation jolted through her. He pushed himself more deeply into her and shuddered with his own powerful release.

Holding him tightly during his climax, Liz squeezed her eyes closed and bit her lip to silence her words of love. She loved him, but even in the drowsy haze that enveloped her following their lovemaking, it seemed that the odds were against them making their relationship permanent. She wouldn't tell him her feelings, wouldn't let it end with those words hanging over them. She burrowed her face in the curve of his neck to hide the tears burning her eyes.

Breathing heavily, Chance struggled to recover both his composure and his strength. He didn't think Liz would be left impressed by his technique if he collapsed to the floor in a tangled heap with her now.

It hadn't really been his intention to take her before she even made it past the front door. But she'd looked so beautiful when she walked in, smiling just for him. He couldn't resist kissing her—and then he couldn't stop. Feeling her legs still locked tightly around his waist, he smiled into her hair, pleased that she'd participated so eagerly in the spontaneous lovemaking. He almost chuckled as he remembered the first time he'd seen her, when he'd wondered if such a beautiful, composed woman was capable of true passion. During the past few days, Liz had shown herself to be more passionate, more responsive, more primitively exciting than any woman he'd ever known.

His feelings for her were more than desire; his hunger was for more than sex. Yet they'd known each other such a short time, and still had so many things to discover about each other before knowing whether what they'd found together would last. But would they make those discoveries or would this mess with his brother and her niece ruin everything between them? And, dammit, what was he supposed to do? Stand back, keep his mouth shut and let Phillip ruin his life?

When he was certain that his legs would support them, Chance drew away from the door, still holding Liz in his arms, her legs still wrapped around him. "Hang on," he muttered, turning toward the bedroom.

She nodded, her arms tightening around his neck.

He tumbled her onto her bed, already reaching for the zipper at the back of her dress, wanting to be rid of that barrier between them. In tandem, Chance tugged at his shirt, stripping it away from him even as he tossed her dress aside. It took him only moments to rid them of the remainder of their clothing. And then his movements slowed, and his touch became lingering.

The first time had been quick, frantic. This time, he intended to savor.

Her scent was delicate, slightly floral. He nuzzled the soft skin beneath her ear. He touched the tip of his tongue to her ear—her taste was as sweet as her scent.

Liz stirred and murmured something incoherent, her palms sliding sensually down his back. He wished he had the words to tell her how much he wanted her, how perfect he found her. He'd never been one to use flowery compliments or endearments, but now, for the first time, he wished that he felt adept at them. Instead, he let his lips and fingertips speak for him. And she trembled at his touch; did that mean she understood his unspoken declarations?

He loved the way she responded to him. A kiss in her palm made her fingers curl. His lips at her wrist had her pulse racing frantically beneath the tender skin. Her nipples drew into tight, pebble-hard peaks when he caressed them; her stomach quivered when he touched her there. And when his fingers slid slowly into the crisp golden curls between her legs, she shuddered, instantly growing hot and wet for him.

Yet he had to talk to her, to make her understand how incredibly special she was to him; how no one before her had ever made him feel quite this much. "Liz," he murmured against her mouth, almost trembling with his urgency. "You're so beautiful. I don't— I feel—"

But the words wouldn't come. Dammit, he simply didn't know how to express what he'd never even felt before. Frustrated, he growled and crushed her mouth beneath his, abandoning the effort. He would tell her in his own way what he wanted her to know.

Confused by Chance's behavior, Liz was tempted to ask him what was bothering him. But before she could, she was so thoroughly overwhelmed that she was capable of doing no more than clinging helplessly to him as he swept her into a storm of passion so wild, so furious, that she wondered if either of them would survive.

She cried out, and Chance groaned when it was over. Propped on his forearms above her to relieve her of his weight, Chance lowered his head wearily, He then rolled onto his side.

"C'mere," he ordered, pulling her close. "I need recovery time before we get up."

"So, who's in a hurry to get up?" she asked, rubbing her cheek affectionately against his sweat-dampened shoulder.

"I couldn't move if I wanted to at the moment, but give me a few minutes and I've gotta find food. I'm starving."

She laughed again. "You're always hungry," she accused him. "It hasn't been that long since lunch."

"It's been five hours!" he protested. "And I just burned a lot of calories. I need sustenance."

"I can't imagine where you put it all," she said in exaggerated wonder. "There's not an extra ounce anywhere on your—"

Her teasing was interrupted by the ringing of the telephone beside the bed. "That will probably be Neal or Sara, letting me know they're back in town."

He nodded grimly, rising slowly to one elbow. "Guess you'd better answer it, then, hadn't you?"

She sighed. "Yes. I suppose I'd better."

Feeling that their beautiful interlude had just come to an end, she lifted the receiver. "Hello."

"We're back!" It was Sara, sounding happy and cheerful. "We had a *wonderful* time."

"I'm glad to hear that," Liz replied, trying very hard to sound casual.

"We brought you a present. Phillip and I are bringing it over now. We'll be there in—oh, twenty minutes, tops. Is that okay?"

"You're coming now?" Liz repeated weakly, her mouth going dry. Chance stiffened beside her.

"Yes. Unless it's a bad time?" Sara asked, suddenly hesitant.

It had to happen eventually. Glancing at Chance's unrevealing expression, Liz said, "No, it's not a bad time. See you in twenty minutes."

"Great. You will clear us with that ferocious security guard, won't you?"

"I have it on the best authority that my security isn't as efficient as it seems," Liz answered wryly, remembering how easily Chance had slipped past the guard Thanksgiving morning. When Sara started to ask for clarification, Liz assured her she'd only been teasing. She hung up a moment later.

"Sara and Phillip are on their way over," she announced, already reaching for her clothes. "We've only got about twenty minutes."

His hand closed over her wrist, holding her still. "Liz?"

She moistened her lips, avoiding his eyes and filled with dread of the evening's outcome. "I have to hurry, Chance. Obviously, we don't want them to guess what we've been doing. And we need to get our stories straight about the weekend. Should we tell them you only arrived today? Act as though we hardly know each other?"

His fingers tightened so abruptly she flinched and murmured a protest. They loosened only fractionally. "Why should we pretend I only arrived today—or that we hardly know each other?" he demanded.

"You were the one who asked me not to mention your presence in Atlanta when they called home," she reminded him.

"Only because I didn't want Phillip to stew about why I was here. I'm not going to lie to him. About anything."

"You're not going to tell them that we—that you and I—?"

"That we're lovers?" Chance eyed her darkly. "Why shouldn't they know?"

"Chance, you can't! I mean— Well, what if you and Phillip quarrel over the engagement? Sara will be terribly hurt if she thinks I agree with you. After all, I owe her a certain amount of loyalty."

"You owe *her* loyalty," Chance repeated, obviously furious. "And what do you owe me, Liz?"

"I owe you nothing!" she replied heatedly, her own anger boiling over. "I told you from the beginning that I wouldn't help you with this."

"You think getting married while she's still just a kid is going to make her happy?" Chance retorted. "Did it make *you* happy, Liz?"

Stung, she jerked her wrist out of his grasp. "That has nothing to do with this," she said haughtily. "I have to get dressed. I'd appreciate it if you'd do the same."

"Fine." He thrust his legs over the side of the bed, scooping up his jeans in the same fluid movement. "God forbid anyone should find out you've been to bed with a hammer jockey, isn't that right, Ms. Society-Wedding Organizer?"

Liz gasped in outrage. "Why, you childish, thick-skulled *male!* Have I *ever* said one word against your occupation? Have I ever acted embarrassed to be with you?"

"Not until now," he answered coolly.

Her fingers tightened on her clothes. "I'm going to get dressed."

"Fine."

"Fine." She marched haughtily to the closet, conscious that it was rather difficult to maintain one's dignity while stark naked. And just as miserably conscious that she'd just badly mishandled that scene with Chance Cassidy.

She'd hurt him by making him think she was ashamed of their affair. She didn't want to hurt him. He'd been hurt enough recently—and probably would be again before the evening was over.

# 8

DURING THE VERY LONG, very quiet, very tense forty-five minute wait for Sara and Phillip, Liz desperately wanted to talk to Chance, to reveal her fears and have him hold her and reassure her that everything would work out.

Instead, she remained silent, checking her appearance every few minutes to make sure her slacks and sweater were straight, her hair neatly combed. It seemed important, for some reason, for her to look composed and confident when she greeted the young couple.

"Aunt Liz!" Sara threw herself into Liz's arms the moment the door opened to her. "We missed you so much. Oh, I wish you could've been with us. We had such a wonderful time. Daddy said to tell you hi and he'll talk to you tomorrow, but he had stuff to do tonight. Wait until you see what we brought you. Phillip, don't stand out there in the hallway. Come in and say hi to Aunt Liz."

"You haven't given me a chance, babe," Phillip replied indulgently, ambling into the apartment with the same easy masculine grace as Chance. Actually, now that she'd met Chance, she saw quite a bit of resemblance between the brothers—dark hair, sharp hazel eyes, crisp profiles. Phillip's features were a bit softer than Chance's, more traditionally handsome. Liz wondered if ten years of outdoor work would have toughened those features to make him even more like his brother.

He kissed her cheek—both he and Sara paying too close attention to her to notice Chance standing in one corner of the room, watching them intently. "How was your weekend, Liz?" Phillip asked politely.

"I guess you could say it was . . . interesting," Liz answered wryly, all too aware of Chance's silent observation. "Phillip—"

Then Sara glimpsed Chance. "Why, hello. Aunt Liz, you didn't say you had company."

Phillip glanced across the room—and froze. "Chance! What—?"

"Chance?" Sara repeated, turning from Chance to Phillip. "Your brother?"

Phillip's expression had turned wary and defiant. "My brother," he confirmed. "What are you doing here, Chance? How long have you been here?"

"I'm here because of your letter, of course," Chance replied smoothly, stepping forward. "I was given Liz's name as a source for locating you. I didn't know you were out of town, of course, since you didn't bother to tell me you were going."

Liz was relieved that he hadn't immediately answered Phillip's question about how long he'd been there, though she knew it would probably come out eventually. She laid a gentle hand on her niece's shoulder. "Chance, this is—"

Phillip stopped her with a quickly upraised hand. "I think I'd like to handle the introductions," he said, his smile faintly apologetic at the interruption. He draped an arm around Sara's shoulders, pulling her away from Liz, facing his brother squarely. "Chance, I'd like you to meet Sara Archer. My fiancée."

After glancing swiftly up at Phillip, as if uncertain how to act, Sara extended a hand to Chance. "It's so nice to meet you, Chance," she said warmly. "Phillip has told me so much about you."

As Chance took Sara's hand, his own swallowing it, he resisted the obvious response that Phillip hadn't told him much of anything about Sara. "It's nice to meet you, too, Sara," he said with a courtesy that Liz found both unexpected and welcoming. She'd been so afraid that he would challenge the engagement immediately. She should have known he'd show a bit more finesse than that.

"This is such a nice surprise," chattered Sara, who tended to be even more talkative than usual when nervous. "Phillip and I were hoping to get to Birmingham soon to meet you and his mother. He was going to call you tonight to make the arrangements."

Chance dropped Sara's hand and glanced at his brother, his polite smile fading. "Were you?"

Phillip swallowed visibly and nodded. "Yeah. I was."

Sara struggled valiantly to keep up her cheery manner. "Would you like to see my ring, Chance?" She held out her left hand. "Isn't it beautiful?"

Liz couldn't quite read the expression that crossed Chance's face when he studied the ring, but he nodded and assured Sara that it was, indeed, a beautiful ring.

"Why don't I get everyone something to drink?" Liz offered quickly, hoping to break the tension in the room. "We can all sit down and talk."

"I was hoping to have a chance to talk to Phillip alone this evening," Chance interjected bluntly. "How about it, Phil? Can you spare me a few minutes later?"

Phillip flinched at the slight dig. "Look, I know you're annoyed that I announced my engagement in a letter instead of in person," he said with a sigh. "It was just that I had so much to tell you and I was afraid I'd forget in the confusion of a phone call. I thought it would be better to tell you everything in the letter and then call tonight and answer any questions you might have. I—uh—I assume you *do* have questions?"

Chance nodded. "I have questions. But they can wait until later," he added, glancing meaningfully at Sara.

"Phillip and I would both be happy to answer your questions, Chance," Sara offered.

"I'd like very much to get to know you better, Sara," Chance said. "I've heard many good things about you, from your aunt and others. But, if you don't mind, I'd like to talk to Phillip alone tonight. Family business."

"I'll be a member of that family in a few months," Sara reminded him, though it was clear that usually daring Sara found her fiancé's older brother intimidating.

"But you're not a member of the family yet," Chance returned gently, his smile pleasant but unrelenting.

Phillip interceded. "Sara, maybe it's best if Chance and I do talk alone this evening. He and I have a lot to discuss."

Sara's lips quivered as she conceded, "All right. If that's what you want, Phillip."

"Thanks, babe. I'll run you home now and give you a call later tonight." He looked back at his brother. "I'll meet you at my place in an hour, okay?"

Chance nodded.

Sara tossed her head. "First I want to give Aunt Liz her present."

"There's no hurry," Chance assured her, crossing his arms over his chest, looking relaxed and patient.

Sara's smile was brittle. "Thank you," she said with pointed politeness. Holding out a small silver-foil box, Sara handed the gift to Liz. "Here it is. Phillip and I picked it out together."

With a strained smile, Liz accepted it. "Why, thank you. It wasn't necessary, but it was sweet of you to think of me."

"Open it," Sara urged.

Liz lifted the lid to peer into the box. "Earrings! They're beautiful," she enthused, lifting one colorful, dangling ornament from the cotton padding. "And so unusual. I've never seen any like them."

"We bought them from an artist who lives near our condo," Sara explained. "She makes the most incredible jewelry you've ever seen. I bought several pieces for myself. But these made me think of you, and Phillip agreed."

"They're lovely," Liz repeated, giving Sara a quick kiss. She smiled at Phillip. "Thank you both."

"You're welcome," Phillip assured her, then looking over at Chance. "We'd better go, Sara. You have an early class in the morning, anyway."

Sara bade Liz an unusually subdued good-night. Noting how worried Sara looked, Liz tried to comfort her with a reassuring smile.

The silence that followed their departure was painfully noticeable. Liz faced Chance, her arms crossed tightly over her chest. "Well, at least you didn't attack them on the spot."

His eyes narrowed. "Did you really think I would?"

"I wouldn't have been surprised."

"I promised you I'd try my best not to hurt your niece. I meant it, Liz. She seems like a nice girl. Very young, but nice."

"She is nice. And, yes, she's young. But she's not a girl, Chance. Don't make the mistake of underestimating her because of her youth."

Chance exhaled impatiently. "Dammit, Liz, this isn't a war! Stop treating me like the enemy."

"You saw Sara and Phillip together. Do you really think he's going to give her up without a fight?"

"I'm not asking him to give her up," he snapped. "How many times do I have to say that? I only want to talk to him about his plans."

"And if he doesn't agree with your suggestions? If he refuses to change his plans?" Liz demanded, watching him closely.

Chance hesitated. "I don't know," he said at length.

Liz didn't back down. "Are you going to accept his right to make his own decisions? Are you going to give him your blessing, attend his wedding, wish him happiness?"

"Dammit, I don't know!" Chance roared, whirling away from her to pace furiously across the room.

"Then I suggest you decide quickly," she advised coolly. "You're supposed to meet Phillip in less than an hour."

Chance took the offensive. "What are you telling me, Liz? You honestly don't think I have the right to express my opinions to my brother, to try to guide him away from what I consider to be a very big mistake?"

"You have the right to your opinions," she answered. "You have the right to express them. You even have the right to ask Phillip to reconsider his plans, particularly his career plans, since you and he have been discussing them for so long. But you don't have the right to try to force him to accept your opinions, or your plans for his future. All you can do is state your case and then let him make his own decisions from there."

His expression closed, Chance nodded. "All right. I've listened to your suggestions. Now you owe me the same courtesy you say I owe Phillip, right? You have to allow me to make my own decision about how to handle this."

Liz swallowed hard. "Of course."

His snort of laughter held little humor. "Yeah, right. I can see you're doing just that."

"I don't know what you mean."

"You're making yourself quite clear, Liz. Either I give my blessing to your niece's wedding, or you and I are through. Isn't that what you're telling me?"

"I never said that," she denied defensively.

"Then, no matter what happens between Phillip and me later, I'm still welcome to come back here to spend the night? You'll take me back into your bed with open arms?"

She didn't like his tone. But, most of all, she didn't like the answer she was forced to give him. "No."

"That's what I thought." He looked furious. Coldly, utterly furious. Like a hard man who'd perceived an ultimatum.

"You don't understand," Liz whispered miserably.

"No?"

"No. It's not your refusal to accept the engagement that would make me reconsider our relationship. It's what that refusal says about you."

"And what is that, Dr. Archer?" he asked with angry mockery.

"That you really are the type of man who thinks he has the right to run the lives of others. I spent two long, miserable, frustrating years with a man like that, Chance. I grew up with a father like that—a man so stubborn, and so convinced of his own wisdom and infallibility, that he drove his son and grandchild away from him and eventually lost his daughter because of that decision. I won't let myself get involved with anyone like that again."

She knew she'd hurt him earlier. Now she could see that she'd hurt him again. For one brief, sharp moment, she wished he'd never come to Atlanta, never walked into her office. Why had he been brought into her life? Why had she been unable to resist falling for him if they were destined to cause each other this kind of pain?

Now totally closed to her, Chance rubbed wearily at the back of his neck. "You know, I thought we'd spent the past few days getting to know each other. Looks like I was wrong. You never got to know me at all." He dropped his hand and turned toward the bedroom. "I'll get my things. And don't worry about your sterling reputation, Liz. I'll let Phillip think you and I are little more than strangers. He should believe it easily enough. That's exactly what we are."

Liz flinched at the parting shot, as well as at the bitterness underlying it. But she didn't cry. She was spared that indignity—at least until after Chance left.

CHANCE HAD TO MAKE a conscious effort to put Liz out of his mind as he faced his brother that evening. The next few minutes had to be handled very carefully; he couldn't afford to be distracted from his conversation with Phillip. He could tell by the wary, suspicious way Phillip was watching him that he'd have to choose his words very carefully. He was glad Phillip's roommate was away for the evening, giving them privacy for their discussion.

"Coffee's good," he said quietly, trying to look at ease as he sat on Phillip's boxy brown sofa, a chipped mug in one hand. "You make it better than I ever have."

"Probably because you always make it strong enough to dissolve paint," Phillip agreed, his smile forced. "I had to learn in self-defense."

"So how are your grades this semester?"

"Still holding on to the four-point average."

"That's good. You must be working hard at it."

"Yeah. You're the one who taught me to give everything my best shot, aren't you?"

"I tried," Chance said with a nod. He took another sip of coffee. "Sara's very pretty."

Phillip's wariness visibly escalated. "She's beautiful," he said. "But that's the least of the reasons why I love her."

"I'm sure she has plenty of admirable qualities. I wouldn't know for certain, of course, since I haven't had the chance to get to know her."

Phillip flushed dully. "That's my fault," he admitted. "I probably should have brought her home to meet you and Mother."

"Why didn't you?"

Phillip shrugged. "It hit me so fast that I was sort of dazed at first. I wanted to make sure of what I was feeling before I brought her home. It took me only a few weeks to know that I wanted to marry her."

"And you didn't think I'd approve, so you delayed telling me," Chance guessed, knowing from Phillip's expression that he was right.

"Yes," his brother confirmed, jaw squared. "I was right, wasn't I?"

"You're twenty-four years old, not even out of school yet, and you've been dating Sara for less than three months. I don't think it's unreasonable for me to worry that you're acting impulsively."

Phillip leaned forward in his chair, facing his older brother squarely, his expression intense and almost desperately earnest. "I knew that's what you'd say, Chance. And I guess I understand why you're worried. But you have to trust me to know what I'm doing. I love Sara with all my heart. I want her to be my wife. I want that more than anything else in the world. Neither of us see any need to wait—to waste any time apart when we've found so much together. Can't you understand that?"

So Liz had been right about Phillip's commitment to Sara. Nothing Chance would say could compete with the all-consuming love blazing in Phillip's eyes when he talked about her. Chance hadn't made a success of his business without learning when to back away, when to change strategies. And, besides, he found that he *could* understand Phillip's feelings for Sara. Maybe he wouldn't have understood a week earlier—but that had been before he'd met Liz.

But he couldn't think about Liz now. Couldn't allow himself to dwell on the pain, the lingering sense of betrayal caused by her comparison of him to her obnoxious ex-husband. He'd have to deal with that later, after he'd reached some agreement with Phillip.

"So you're getting married," he said.

"Yes." Phillip relaxed only fractionally, obviously knowing what would come. "I'm getting married. At the end of June."

"Congratulations."

"Thank you."

"Why didn't you try to give her the ring?" Chance asked, a question that had been nagging at him ever since Sara had shown him her modest engagement ring.

Phillip looked surprised. "Great-Grandmother's ring?"

Chance nodded. "It was intended for the next Cassidy bride. I would have expected you to ask for it."

"But— Well, I always thought the ring was meant for your wife," Phillip explained. "You're the eldest, and you're the one named after our great-grandfather. It never crossed my mind to ask for it."

Chance was touched by Phillip's sincerity. "The ring belongs as much to you as it does to me," he conceded reluctantly, though he wanted with all his being to deny the words. Still, despite his initial objection to Sara Archer's wearing the Cassidy ring, Chance couldn't have refused Phillip if he'd asked. His honor and his sense of obligation to family were both too strong. "If you want Sara to wear it—"

"Sara has a ring," Phillip cut in firmly. "She and I picked it out together, after looking at hundreds of others. The Cassidy ring should go to your wife, if she wants it."

"Yeah. Well, I haven't got a wife." Liz's image flashed vividly across his mind before he ruthlessly pushed it away. "The way things have been going, I may never have one."

"Oh, I doubt that," Phillip said with a faint smile. "You've got a stronger sense of family than anyone I've ever known. You won't ever be totally content until you have a wife and a couple of little Cassidys to raise."

But Chance wasn't there to talk about his own future, and both of them knew it. Though he was unwillingly intrigued by his brother's words, Chance ignored them for now. "Your engagement isn't the only reason I'm here, you know," he said quietly.

Phillip's smile faded, his expression turning grim. "I know."

Chance set his half-emptied mug on a low table at his elbow, framing his words carefully in his mind. "You disappointed me, Phillip," he said at last, gently, so that the words were not an attack, but an unhappy statement of fact.

"I know, Chance. I'm sorry," Phillip said, sounding penitent.

"We deserved more than a letter. For God's sake, Phillip, if not for me, for Mother. Don't you know how you hurt her?"

"I'm sorry. I shouldn't— I wasn't—" He paused for a deep breath. "I guess I wasn't really thinking enough about Mother when I sent the letter," he admitted. "I was thinking of you."

"So you said," Chance acknowledged. "You didn't think I'd approve, so you wanted to make all your arguments without interruption. That makes sense, I guess. But it doesn't make what you did any less thoughtless or selfish."

"I know. I'm sorry," Phillip muttered, unable to meet his brother's eyes now.

"At least have the guts to admit you knew it wasn't your engagement I'd have the most trouble accepting. Oh, you were convinced I'd think you're too young, that you've been carried away by infatuation. But you also knew I'd accept your ultimate right to make that decision—that mistake, perhaps—on your own. Didn't you?"

Phillip nodded, staring at his hands.

"I won't lie to you, Phil. I think you should wait to get married. I think you should be out of school for a while, experience life a bit more before tying yourself down to a family. But I can't stop you, and I won't try."

"Thanks, Chance."

Chance nodded shortly, his voice hardening as he went on. "But this job with Neal Archer— Dammit, you had no right to accept that offer without talking to me first, Phillip. You and I had an agreement, a plan we made years ago. You owed your loyalty to that prior commitment, but you acted as though it never existed."

"Chance, I know you're disappointed—"

"Disappointed?" Chance broke in curtly. "It's more than that, Phillip. I'm stunned. I'm hurt. But, most of all, I'm furious that you think you can just push me aside like an inconvenient stranger now that you've had what you consider to be a better offer from your girlfriend's father."

"Chance, it's not like that—"

"You know, all those years when you were growing up, I tried to instill a sense of values in you. I tried to be for you what Dad was for me—someone to show you how to go on in the world, teach you about responsibility and commitment and a man's honor. I thought I'd done a pretty good job. I was so goddamned proud of you. I had so much invested in you. And then this happened."

Deathly pale now, Phillip managed to meet Chance's eyes. "I'll repay every penny you spent on my education, Chance. I've always planned to do that."

Cursing savagely, Chance surged to his feet. He was getting damned sick and tired of people misjudging him, he decided. "I wasn't talking about monetary investment, Phillip," he said coldly. "You know full well that I never considered your education a burden—or a loan. What little Dad had to leave us belonged to both of us, and he wanted you to be provided for, wanted you to have all the advantages of a good education."

"Which you denied yourself so you could take care of Mother and me," Phillip pointed out softly.

"I've done all right for myself."

"Better than all right. You built a successful company out of virtually nothing, turning Cassidy Construction into one of the biggest and best-known construction firms in Alabama. You've made a lot of money—enough to take excellent care of Mother for the rest of her life and to put me through six years of college. But Cassidy Construction was *your* dream, Chance, not mine."

"Since when?" Chance demanded, fists doubled on his hips. "You always said you were looking forward to working with me when you graduated. Were you lying to me all those years, saying what you thought I wanted to hear until after I'd financed your education?"

"No!" Stung, Phillip surged to his feet, standing almost toe-to-toe with his brother in a pose so similar that it might have been amusing to an outside observer. "You know that's not true!"

"How could I know it?"

"Because you know *me*, dammit! I never used you like that, Chance—I never would."

"Then why this sudden change of heart? Why is Cassidy Construction suddenly *my* dream and Archer Industries yours? Why are all our plans shot to hell now, when they were so damned close to taking place?"

"Chance, I didn't plan this," Phillip said pleadingly. "I've always known how much you wanted me to join you—and I thought it was what I wanted, too. I tried so damned hard to want it as much as you did. But during the past year—maybe longer—I've known, deep inside, that I was deceiving you, trying to deceive myself.

"And then I met Sara and Neal, and I spent some time with them, learning about his company, his plans for the future of the industry—and I felt as though I'd found the niche that's been waiting for me since I was born. I know it sounds stupid. Fanciful or sappy or whatever you might call it. But it's true."

Chance felt as though he'd taken a blow to the chest—several of them, in fact. "Why didn't you tell me you'd started to feel that way?" he asked heavily, his voice strained.

"I couldn't," Phillip whispered. "I didn't want to hurt you."

"So you wrote me a letter."

Phillip winced. "That was a mistake. A stupid, thoughtless one. I guess I knew even when I mailed it that I was being a coward."

Chance pushed his hands into the pockets of his jeans, feeling suddenly... old. And tired. "You're sure this is what you want?"

"I'm sure," Phillip said regretfully. "I'm sorry, Chance. But this is what I want."

"Then I won't try to stop you. I won't hold you to your commitment to me."

"I—" Phillip's voice broke. And he suddenly looked very young, and a little scared. But both of them knew there was no going back. Not now.

"I'm not going to let this destroy our family," Chance said, recalling Liz's warnings, the unhappiness in her eyes when she'd talked of her own family's estrangement. "You are still my brother. I—uh— Well, you know."

His eyes moist, Phillip attempted a smile. "I know. I love you, too, Chance." It had always been easier for Phillip to express his feelings.

"You'll come home for Christmas," Chance ordered gruffly, edging toward the door. "Bring Sara with you. Neal, too, if he'll come. We need to get to know each other, since we're going to be related. Explain to them that Mother isn't able to travel."

"I'll discuss it with them," Phillip promised. "I'm sure they'll agree. Both of them have said they want to get to know my family."

"I'll tell Mother. She'll be pleased."

"I'm sorry I missed spending Thanksgiving with the two of you. It was the first time we haven't been together on Thanksgiving, wasn't it?"

Chance didn't answer, since he wasn't ready for Phillip to know that he hadn't been home for Thanksgiving, either. "I'd better be going."

"Where are you staying tonight?"

"I think I'll head on home."

"Tonight?" Phillip looked down at his watch in concern. "Shouldn't you get some rest first?"

"I'm not tired," Chance lied. "I'll be fine." After the emotional confrontations with Liz and Phillip, Chance wasn't sure he'd ever sleep peacefully again. He knew he wouldn't tonight, anyway. He'd rather be on the road than staring at the ceiling of some motel room.

Phillip tried again to change Chance's mind, but gave up when he saw it wasn't going to work, urging him, instead, to drive safely.

"I will," Chance replied, one hand on the doorknob. "Oh, and Phillip—"

"Yes?"

He'd wanted to leave a message for Liz. Now he had no idea what he wanted to say to her. "Never mind. I'll talk to you later."

Phillip agreed, looking rather relieved that everything was finally out in the open between them and that nothing disastrous had happened as a result.

Chance climbed slowly into the cab of his truck. He didn't share Phillip's youthful optimism. As far as Chance was concerned, nothing would ever be the same after these past five days in Atlanta.

# 9

SARA LEANED EAGERLY over Devon's shoulder as Devon sketched on a large pad. Liz watched from Devon's other side, as fascinated as her niece by the process of designing a personalized wedding gown. Discarded sketches on crumpled sheets lay around them in Devon's office.

"Yes, that's the neckline I wanted!" Sara squealed excitedly, almost dropping the stack of bridal magazines from which she had chosen individual elements she particularly liked for her gown.

"That's a portrait neckline," Devon explained, adding detail to the crisp, shawl-like collar of the gown in the sketch. "We can drop it down to a V in front with a lace rosette, if you like. Or maybe a pearl cluster."

"I like the rosette," Sara decided.

Devon drew it in, her pencil skimming swiftly over the paper. "We can leave your arms bare or add a gauntlet sleeve beneath the collar," she murmured, concentrating on her work.

"Bare," Sara and Liz said in unison. They laughed at the coincidence, which wasn't the first time they'd automatically agreed on details. Their tastes were amazingly similar at times.

"With long, lace gloves," Sara added.

Liz smiled. "Of course."

Devon drew a tight bodice, delicate lines indicating lace brought to a point in front. Beneath the Basque waistline, a full skirt fell in three tiers, draping to a chapel-length train. "How about a bow here?" she asked, indicating the derriere area.

"A peplum," Sara said instead. "I love peplums."

Liz and Devon both frowned. "A peplum?" Devon asked doubtfully. "Are you sure?"

"With this dress?" Liz eyed the sketch. "I don't think you're going to like it, Sara."

"Sure I will. I love peplums," Sara repeated, her characteristic stubbornness kicking in—not for the first time since they'd started planning her wedding. It was the second week of December, and Sara acted as though she had only a few days to complete her plans, though the wedding wasn't scheduled until late June. It was a reaction Liz had seen many times before from anxious, excited brides-to-be.

"But with the tiers and the collar—"

"Aunt Liz," Sara wailed, "I know what I like."

Devon gave Liz a minute shake of her head, indicating she'd handle the problem later. Liz was sure she would. Devon had yet to design a gown that wasn't near perfect in every detail. Sometimes the brides had to be persuaded that the changes were their own ideas, but Devon had an almost-infallible knack for gentle diplomacy.

"I'll have completed sketches ready for you in a few weeks," Devon assured Sara. "I'll sketch the dress in detail from all angles, so you'll know exactly how it will look. The attendants' dresses, too, of course."

Sara smiled happily. "I can't wait to see them. I know Aunt Liz and my girlfriends are going to look gorgeous in their attendants' dresses."

"Aunt Liz is going to look very old, standing with those twenty-year-old college girls," Liz grumbled, rolling her eyes at Devon's snicker of response. "Are you sure you wouldn't be content just to have me organize your wedding, Sara? I really have to participate in it, as well?"

"I want you for my maid of honor," Sara asserted, smiling. "You'll be the most beautiful member of the party."

Liz kissed Sara's cheek. "Hardly. Besides, the bride is always the most beautiful."

"And you won't be the oldest person up there, anyway," Sara added with tactless ingenuity. "Phillip's having Chance for his best man and he's two years older than you are."

It was all Liz could do to keep from flinching at the sound of Chance's name, even after two weeks of hearing Sara say it in artless conversations—two weeks during which Liz hadn't heard a word from Chance.

As though sensing her friend's anguish, Devon surreptitiously touched Liz's hand in a soft, fleeting touch—an I'm-here-for-you touch. Liz managed a smile, though she didn't know how natural it looked to her two sharp-eyed observers. She thanked the stars that Sara had been too wrapped up in her own plans to notice her aunt's precarious moods during the past two weeks.

Oblivious to the undercurrents between Liz and Devon, Sara chattered on. "Phillip was so pleased when Chance agreed to be his best man. Chance still isn't really happy about the wedding, I'm afraid, but Phillip assures me he'll come around. He says Chance has always been sort of overprotective and he's worried that Phillip and I are too young and that we haven't known each other long enough. I guess I can understand that. After all, Chance hasn't had the chance—gosh, that sounds funny, doesn't it?—Chance hasn't had the *opportunity*—that's better—to get to know me. I'm sure that when he spends more time with me he'll realize that I'm very mature and responsible and I'll make a perfect wife for Phillip."

Liz choked dramatically, proud of her success in hiding the pain that ripped through her with each mention of Chance's name.

Sara responded to her aunt's teasing with a reproachful look. "You're saying I'm *not* mature and responsible?" she demanded, her hands on her slender hips.

Liz chuckled and gave her niece a hug. "Of course, you are, Sara. I was only joking."

"Then I forgive you," Sara assured her with royal haughtiness. And then she laughed musically. "You're so funny, Aunt Liz."

Liz thought of the old song, "The Tears of a Clown." Like the clown in the tune, she'd been hiding her tears of the past two weeks until she was alone.

A doorbell chimed from somewhere behind them. Sara jumped up. "I'm sure that's Phillip. Don't let him see the sketches!"

Devon laughed softly. "We won't let him see the sketches."

"I don't want him to know anything about the dress," Sara emphasized. "I want it to be a total surprise when I come down the aisle."

"Of course."

Phillip greeted Liz with his usual affection, Devon with easy courtesy and Sara with a loving kiss. "Ready to go to Bobbi's house?" he asked her. "It's an early Christmas party," he explained to Liz and Devon. "Bobbi's leaving for Colorado next week."

"Phillip, wait until you see my dress!" Sara told him, clutching his arm in excitement. "I'll have a portrait neckline with a rosette and a big, full skirt with . . ."

She was still describing the dress—in minute detail—when she and Phillip left.

Devon looked quizzically at Liz and then burst out laughing. "I thought she wanted it to be a secret," she said.

Liz smiled broadly. "Sara can't keep a minor secret," she explained. "Neal and I learned long ago not to tell her what we'd gotten anyone for Christmas or birthdays because it just seems to leap right out of her mouth at the first opportunity. Fortunately, she manages not to divulge anything that really is crucially confidential. I could tell her a personal problem, for example, and be certain that she wouldn't betray my confidence."

"And speaking of personal problems . . ." Devon began smoothly, turning to lay a hand on Liz's arm. "Do you want to talk now?"

Liz sighed. "I haven't been fooling you a bit, have I?"

"With your smiling and teasing? No. I can tell you're hurting. Is there anything I can do to help?"

"Not really. But thanks, Devon."

Looking concerned, Devon gently urged her toward the kitchen. "Let's have a cup of coffee and talk, okay?"

Liz managed a smile. "That sounds good."

"So Chance has decided not to protest the wedding?" Devon asked fifteen minutes later when she and Liz were settled at her cozy kitchen table with their coffee. "I mean, if he's agreed to serve as best man, he's not boycotting the ceremony or anything."

Liz nodded. "Evidently he and Phillip came to some sort of agreement the night Chance left town. Phillip told Neal that Chance made it quite clear that he thinks Phillip should wait before getting married, but if he's determined to go through with it, Chance won't try to stop him."

"Were you surprised?"

"Yes," Liz answered candidly. "To be honest, I was. I really thought he was going to forbid Phillip to go through with the plans, stage a dramatic scene."

"The way your parents would have done," Devon said perceptively.

"Yes," Liz admitted, uncomfortably remembering Chance's accusations that she was determined to think the worst of him. Perhaps she had been.

"And what about the job Phillip's taking with Neal?"

Liz sipped her coffee, then lowered the cup carefully to the table. "Evidently that's still a sore subject. Neal said that Phillip had an almost haunted look in his eyes when he mentioned that part of the confrontation. Phillip said Chance has accepted Phillip's right to make the choice, but that Chance still feels betrayed by that choice. Neal keeps assuring Phillip that Chance will get over it, that they can all be relieved Chance is willing to accept Phillip's decisions without allowing it to destroy their relationship as brothers."

"I'm glad Chance is being reasonable about it," Devon said. "It would have broken Sara's heart if she'd come between Phillip and his family."

Liz nodded. "Yes, it would."

Devon cleared her throat and looked studiously into her coffee cup. "Chance hasn't called you?"

Liz flinched. "No."

"Do you have any idea why?"

Miserably, Liz nodded. "We said some pretty heated things that last night. I compared him to my father and ex-husband and he accused me of being a snob who didn't want to be involved with a man who owns a construction company."

"He was wrong about you. Maybe you were just as wrong about him?" Devon asked, raising her eyes to Liz's troubled face.

"Maybe," Liz agreed, remembering how startled she'd been to learn that Chance had apparently behaved quite reasonably during his discussion with Phillip. She'd been so sure that he'd handle the scene badly, end up losing his temper—and losing his brother. Instead, he'd stated his case and then accepted Phillip's decision, if not eagerly, at least cordially. He'd even invited Sara and Neal to spend Christmas in Birmingham so the two families could become better acquainted.

She'd underestimated him. Or maybe—just maybe—some of what she'd said during their weekend together had gotten through. Maybe he'd seen the wisdom in her advice. Maybe he wasn't as unbending, inflexible and dictatorial as she'd thought he was.

But he still hadn't called her, so he clearly hadn't forgiven her for the things she'd said, for the suspicions she'd harbored about him. Or maybe he'd never really foreseen a future for them. Maybe he'd never envisioned any more for them than a passionate weekend affair. Although he had once mentioned a future, she remembered wistfully—a camping trip, he'd said. Had he spoken impulsively, in the aftermath of sexual satisfaction, only to regret or even forget the words later? Or *had* he—?

"Liz?"

Realizing she'd been deep in her own thoughts for several long, silent moments, Liz looked up apologetically. "Sorry, Devon. What were you saying?"

"Have you—um—thought of calling him?"

"No." She lied, of course. She'd thought so many times of calling him. But each time she'd almost convinced herself to do so she remembered the look in his eyes, could almost hear him referring to them as little more than strangers. How could she call him after that?

"Are you sure there's nothing I can do? I hate seeing you look so sad."

Liz shook her head. "Just be my friend."

"Always." Devon smiled bracingly. "You'd rather talk about something else, wouldn't you?"

Liz nodded fervently. "Please."

Devon complied, which was one of the many reasons Liz liked the other woman so much. Devon always seemed to know just what Liz needed—whether it was to talk about her problems or to be pleasantly distracted from them. "Liz, you have *got* to do something about your niece," Devon lectured solemnly.

Liz cooperated willingly. "What, exactly, do you want me to do about Sara?"

"It's this out-of-the-blue plan of hers to fix me up with her father! Why, after knowing me for several years, has she suddenly decided she wants me for a stepmother? And what will I have to do to convince her that I really don't want to be placed in an embarrassing situation with your brother? Like—" she shuddered delicately "—an arranged date. Arranged by Sara, that is."

Liz winced in sympathy. "I understand. Sara can be a little frightening when she becomes obsessed with an idea. She's decided that Neal's going to be lonely after she gets married, and she wants to make sure he has someone. I suppose you should be flattered that she thinks you're good enough for her adored father. There have been a couple of women over the years who would have liked Sara's approval—she despised them."

"Okay, I'm flattered. But I'm also terrified. I have this fear that she's going to be calling me 'Mom' before I've spoken more than a few words to Neal. Honestly, Liz, I think she has it envisioned in that convoluted mind of hers."

Liz smiled. "You may be right."

"Well, try to stop her, will you? Tell her I'm really not as nice as I seem. Tell her I'm a closet kleptomaniac or something."

She couldn't help laughing. "Honestly, Devon, no one would ever believe you're anything but what you seem to be. Very nice."

Devon sighed despondently. "Terminally nice," she grumbled.

"Why have you taken such exception to that word lately?" Liz asked, amused by the disgust on Devon's pretty face.

"Nice? It's just so—so bland. It sounds like something Brandy would say to me as an insult."

"Only because your younger sister is determined to make everyone think she's wild and wicked," Liz countered.

Nodding, Devon made a face. "I don't know what we're going to do with her," she complained. "She's getting worse all the time. But sometimes I wonder if she's right about me—if I really am duller than dishwater."

"Don't be ridiculous," Liz argued loyally. "Brandy's just jealous of your success with your designing. You're a wonderful person, Devon Fleming, and I'm proud to be your friend."

"Well, yes, but then you're duller than dishwater, yourself," Devon added sadly.

Liz gasped, then laughed until her sides hurt. "Honestly, Devon," she said when she could speak steadily. "That sneaky sense of humor of yours really gets to me sometimes. Maybe I'll help Sara fix you up with Neal. I think I'd like having you for a sister-in-law."

Looking horrified, Devon held up her hands in surrender. "No, please. Not that."

Her grin fading to a soft smile, Liz looked affectionately across the table. "Thanks, Dev. I needed that."

"Hey, any time you need an insult, you know where to find me."

Liz chuckled and rose to rinse her coffee cup. "You know exactly what I mean. But now I have to go. I've got a zillion things to do this evening."

"Me, too. But I'm glad you came with Sara for our first session. It was nice to have a chance to talk to you. We've both been so busy lately."

"It's always hectic this close to Christmas," Liz commented. "It'll be nice when the holidays are over and life gets back to normal, won't it?"

"Very," Devon agreed.

They parted with fond hugs and promises to get together again as soon as they could. As she walked outside to her car, Liz wondered how it was possible to hurt so much inside and yet manage to laugh at her friend's teasing. Was her now familiar, now constant pain something she was going to have to live with for the rest of her life?

CHANCE STOOD BESIDE his bed, the small carved wooden box in his hand, open. He stared for a long time at the ring inside it. Funny, he'd always had a vague mental image of the woman who'd wear that ring someday. The fantasy woman had borne little resemblance to Elizabeth Archer. And yet, now, he found it hard to imagine anyone else wearing it.

With a grumble of self-disgust, he closed the box, tossing it onto his dresser. Dammit, what was wrong with him lately? Business was booming, causing him to work backbreaking hours, and as much as he worried about Phillip, and Nadine hadn't been feeling well—all he could really seem to think about was Liz. Thoughts of her hovered constantly in the back of his mind, whether he was working or resting, with others or alone—and at night, especially at night, when he lay alone in his bed.

He hadn't stopped wanting her. In fact, he was almost ready to admit that he needed her. And that admission shook him, for he was very much afraid he would never have her.

He shoved his hand through his hair and turned away from the bed, looking unenthusiastically at the adjoining bathroom. He needed a shower. Something to eat. He'd worked late tonight and Nadine was already in bed, so he'd be eating alone. The prospect didn't excite him.

*He could call her.*

The thought crossed his mind so quickly, so unexpectedly, that he found himself reaching for the bedside phone almost before he knew what he was doing. He clenched his fingers and pulled his arm back to his side. What would he say? Would she even want to hear from him? Was what they'd had really as momentous as it had seemed? Or had they both been carried away by circumstances, proximity?

Had he really fallen in love in only a few days' time, after waiting nearly thirty-four years to do so?

He remembered the quarrel, remembered the pain. But most of all, he remembered the loving. With sudden determination, he picked up the phone.

LIZ WAS DOING HER NAILS, trying to concentrate on anything other than Chance, when the telephone rang. Careful not to smudge the three mauve-painted fingers of her right hand, she lifted the receiver to her ear. "Hello?"

In the brief, taut silence that followed, she stiffened, somehow knowing who was at the other end even before he spoke. "Hi, Liz."

"Chance," she whispered, her hands beginning to tremble.

"Yeah." He paused again, as if even he wasn't quite sure why he'd called.

"I—didn't expect to hear from you," Liz said.

"You should have," he replied surprisingly. "Did I call at a bad time?"

"No." She cleared her throat, unable to resist asking, "Why *did* you call?"

"I want you to come with Sara and your brother to Birmingham for Christmas."

She certainly hadn't expected that. She'd thought she'd be spending another holiday alone. Now she didn't quite know what to say except, "Why?"

"Because your niece is marrying into my family, which makes you a part of the family, as well. Because Nadine wants a chance to get to know the people who are important to Phillip, since she won't be able to travel to Atlanta, even for the wedding. But mostly because I want to see you again. I need to see you, Liz."

Forgetting the sticky nail polish, she gripped the receiver more tightly. "You do?"

"Yes. Will you come?"

"Yes," she heard herself say without really thinking about her answer.

"Good." He sounded satisfied—and relieved. "So I'll see you then."

"Yes. Thanks for asking me."

"Thanks for accepting. Good night, Liz."

She noted that he didn't say good-bye. Neither did she. "Good night, Chance."

She inhaled shakily, staring in numb bemusement at the splotches of mauve on her palm, where three freshly painted fingernails had dug shallow half-moon indentations into her skin.

A sudden surge of panic almost made her snatch up the phone and call Chance back, tell him she'd made a mistake and couldn't come for Christmas, after all. She could say she was simply too busy, that she wanted to spend Christmas in Atlanta with her friends. Or she could tell him the truth: that she was terrified of facing him again, loving him, wanting him, and so afraid they'd only end up hurting each other again.

But she wouldn't call him—because she'd been so utterly miserable during the past weeks; because she wanted to see him so badly she ached with it. She would spend Christmas with Chance.

# 10

"SURE YOU'VE GOT everything you want to take with you?" Neal asked one last time, as he and Liz prepared to leave her apartment on Monday, December 23. Sara and Phillip were to meet them at the airport for the holiday trip to Birmingham.

"I think so." Liz looked around the apartment with a frown, running through a mental checklist. The stove was off, thermostat set, answering machine on. She thought she'd packed everything she'd need for the five days they would spend in Birmingham.

Five days with Chance, she thought with a tiny shiver of mingled dread and anticipation. Five days with him—and his stepmother, his brother, her brother and her niece. Heaven help her.

"Liz?" Neal prodded. "Ready to go?"

She drew a deep, bracing breath and reached for her coat. "Yes. I'm ready."

Neal carried her bags down and stowed them in the trunk of the car, along with his own. He snapped the trunk shut and rounded the Mercedes sedan to climb behind the wheel. "I can't believe I let Sara talk me into this," he said as he started the engine.

Liz looked at him sympathetically, knowing how reluctant Neal had been to spend five days with strangers—particularly during the holidays. He had refused to stay at the Cassidy home, preferring, instead, to make reservations for himself and Liz at an exclusive hotel close by. Liz had approved heartily of that plan.

At least a dozen times during the past week she'd changed her mind about accompanying her family to Birmingham. She'd told herself she should get over Chance Cassidy, put him out of her mind—and her heart. She'd almost convinced herself that she could have done so by June, by the time she saw him again at Sara's wedding. But even as those thoughts crossed her mind, she knew she wouldn't be over Chance by June. She wasn't sure she'd *ever* be over Chance.

Oh, yes, she certainly understood Neal's hesitation to make this trip. She felt exactly the same way, though for entirely different reasons.

"It means a lot to Sara that we're going," Liz reminded Neal, knowing that was the only argument that really mattered to him. It had always been hard for Neal to refuse Sara anything that she truly wanted. "And to Phillip, of course, since his mother is unable to travel to meet us."

Neal smiled briefly, "Phillip's a nervous wreck over this visit. I think he's worried that his brother and I will get into it over the job thing. Damn, I wish Phillip had told me earlier that he'd had a verbal agreement to work with Cassidy after his graduation."

"Would knowing that have stopped you from offering Phillip a position?" Liz asked, curious.

Neal hesitated, then ruefully shook his head. "No. Phillip's got a lot to offer my company. And it's been obvious all along that he really wants to give it a shot. But maybe I'd have urged him to handle things differently with his family. He didn't do that very well."

"Yes, well, you'd have been speaking from the experience that Phillip hasn't had enough years to develop," Liz pointed out. "But it's not your fault he didn't tell you."

"What's Chance really like?" Neal questioned, slanting Liz a careful look. "You've never given me much of an answer when I've asked you before."

Liz could picture Chance as clearly as if he stood in front of her, though it had been almost a month since she'd seen him. She could hear him with painful clarity—talking, laughing, murmuring in the darkness. If she closed her eyes and concentrated, she could almost feel his callused, yet surprisingly gentle hands on her skin. But she found him almost impossible to describe.

"He's—a lot like you in some ways," she said finally, slowly. "Quiet and serious but with an underlying sense of humor. Headstrong and almost arrogantly confident of his own abilities." She didn't add that both men had their hidden insecurities—Chance, his discomfort over his lack of a college education in a degree-conscious business world, and Neal, the painful disenchantment and self-imposed isolation resulting from his youthful mistake.

Though apparently taken aback by her way of describing Chance, Neal seemed even more intrigued. "You know, you never really said exactly how long he was in Atlanta before we got back from Florida. Had he just arrived that morning?"

Liz squirmed restlessly beneath her seat belt. She'd been relieved that no one had thought to ask this question before, but she should have known it would occur to Neal eventually. So little escaped her perceptive brother. "No," she answered quietly, unable—and unwilling—to lie to him. "He'd been in town a few days, waiting for Phillip."

"A few days?"

"Since the day before Thanksgiving," Liz admitted in a low tone.

Neal frowned thoughtfully. "Chance Cassidy was in Atlanta for five days before we came home?"

"Yes."

"You spent some time with him during those days?"

"Some, yes." Had he asked, she could have told him the exact number of hours she'd spent with Chance. "We had dinner a few times, saw a movie. And—um—we went fishing on Sunday."

The car swerved, though Neal quickly brought it back under control. "You went—fishing?" he repeated carefully.

"Yes. I even caught a few."

"Why didn't you mention this before?"

"No one asked," Liz prevaricated, knowing even as she said it that Neal would never let her get away with it.

She was right, of course. "Elizabeth." He only called her by her first name when he was annoyed with her. "Just what went on with you and Chance Cassidy, anyway? Why did he call you with a personal invitation to Birmingham two weeks after he invited the rest of us? Have the two of you been in contact ever since he left?"

"No," Liz answered hastily. "We've only talked that one time since he went home."

Neal took the exit for the airport, moving skillfully through the heavy traffic. Her brother sensed something had happened that had changed her life forever, Liz realized nervously, her hands twisting in her lap.

"Chance Cassidy came to Atlanta to try to put an end to his brother's engagement, didn't he?" Neal asked.

"I think he did," Liz agreed.

"And you talked him out of it? Convinced him to express his concerns and then stand back and let Phillip and Sara decide for themselves?"

"I advised him not to do anything that would permanently alienate Phillip. Chance made up his own mind how to handle the confrontation."

"So why'd you go fishing with him?"

"Why not? He asked, it sounded like fun, so I went. We had a good time." She remembered the laughter.

And she remembered the passion after she'd administered first aid to the scratch on his neck. A wave of longing swept through her—so intense that she quivered, though she hoped Neal wouldn't notice.

"Why are you so curious about what I did with Chance Cassidy?" she demanded, deciding to turn the questioning back to Neal before his inquiries became even more personal.

Neal risked a quick glance at her. "I guess I've been so busy with Sara and the business that I've been a little slow when it came to you. I've noticed you were troubled about something, could tell you'd been upset by something, but it only now occurred to me that Phillip's brother had anything to do with it. Did he do something—say something—to hurt you? Did the two of you quarrel? Is that why he was worried that you wouldn't come unless he persuaded you with a personal call?"

"We did quarrel," Liz admitted reluctantly. "Just before he left."

"About Sara and Phillip?"

"In a way." How could she explain that they'd quarreled about Sara and Phillip only as symbols of their real problems—her fear that he was too controlling, too domineering; his, that she was a snob who couldn't accept his working-class background or his simple, less-than-elegant life-style?

"Dammit, Liz, why won't you talk to me about this? What aren't you telling me?"

Liz drew a deep breath. "Anything I'm not telling you really has nothing to do with you, Neal," she said as gently as she could and still stand firm. "It's between Chance and me."

Neal wasn't deterred by her stern tone. But then, she never had been able to intimidate her older brother. Nor had she ever been able to fully convince him that his overly protective interference wasn't always welcome, or even necessary. "So you are involved with him," he said.

"Neal . . ."

"I won't push you," Neal muttered disgruntledly. "But if he has hurt you, or if he does anything to hurt you while we're in Birmingham, I want to know about it."

Liz didn't answer, since she couldn't be absolutely certain that she wouldn't be hurt during the visit to Birmingham. She only knew that she would try her best to hide it from Neal if she was. There was absolutely no way that she would cause a family quarrel now that Chance had made the effort to meet Phillip and Sara halfway.

BY THE TIME the short flight from Atlanta to Birmingham came to an end, Liz felt as though her insides had been tied into a tight knot. It was almost impossible to take a deep breath. One hand on her nervous stomach, she wished she'd worn something looser than the snug-waisted berry-red dress she'd chosen in deference to the season.

As though he sensed her turmoil, Neal placed a supportive hand at the small of her back as they followed Sara and Phillip off the plane into the air terminal. Liz tried to smile at him, but knew the attempt was shaky at best.

Chance was waiting for them.

Surrounded by crowds of noisily greeting holiday travelers, Chance was conspicuous for his stillness and sobriety. He stood unmoving while his guests approached, his eyes focusing unwaveringly on Liz. His hair was longer than it had been when she'd seen him last, as though he'd been too busy to have it trimmed since then. He wore his usual outfit of close-fitting jeans, white oxford-cloth shirt and battered brown leather jacket. Liz thought he was the sexiest man she'd ever seen.

Phillip greeted his brother with a quick, self-conscious hug. "Hi, Chance. Thanks for picking us up."

Sara gave Chance her warmest, brightest smile. She was determined to make Phillip's brother love her—as everyone else who knew her eventually did. She rose on tiptoe to press a kiss to Chance's hard, tanned cheek. "It was so sweet of you to have us all for Christmas," she said. "I just know it's going to be a wonderful holiday. I'd like you to meet my father, Neal Archer. Daddy, this is Chance."

Removing his hand from Liz's waist to extend it to Chance, Neal smiled politely, his sharp dark eyes studying Chance. Chance took the offered hand with an equally polite, equally forced smile. Watching them, Liz was struck again by the similarity between them. Not in appearance, exactly, but in the way they held their heads, the look of proven competence in their eyes. They were two men who knew a great deal about responsibility, self-sacrifice, hard work.

Liz suspected Chance would be surprised if she told him how much he and Neal were alike. The plumber's son and the maverick scion of a distinguished old-money family. Two very strong, occasionally hard, and unapologetically stubborn men.

Chance's eyes met Liz's. He held out his hand to her. "Hello, Liz. It's good to see you again."

His words were merely courteous, his tone distantly friendly. But in his eyes she read a message that sent a tremor all the way through her. When his fingers tightened around hers, she knew he'd felt it, too.

"Hello, Chance," she said, hoping she camouflaged her tumultuous emotions as successfully as he had. "Thank you for inviting me."

His smile was just faintly mocking. "My pleasure."

"I've rented a car for your use this week," Chance informed Neal. "Your hotel's within a couple of miles of my place, so it'll be easy enough for you to find your way around if you aren't familiar with the city."

"Thanks, Chance. That was very thoughtful of you."

Chance inclined his head, restless to be under way. "The baggage area's this way," he said, gesturing with his right arm.

As she walked between Phillip and Neal, Sara's nervous excitement was evident in her animated face. When Liz was jostled by a rushing passenger as they left the terminal, Chance reached out to steady her. Yet as Liz felt his fingers firmly gripping her arm, she realized there was nothing casual about his touch. Certainly there was nothing casual about her reaction to it.

CHANCE LIVED IN A tasteful, ranch-style house in a quiet, upper-middle-class neighborhood. It wasn't as large or impressive as Neal's Tudor or the even more imposing mansion Liz had grown up in, but she liked Chance's house. It looked . . . like a home, she decided, studying it with pleasure.

His manner more gruff than usual, Chance led them inside and straight to the living room, where Nadine waited eagerly to greet them.

Liz thought Nadine looked like the emotional type who'd burst into tears at the drop of a lace handkerchief, but she was drawn to the glow of genuine sweetness in Nadine's soft blue eyes.

Phillip obviously loved his mother very much, despite the thoughtless manner in which he had handled the announcement of his engagement. But it was Chance's behavior toward Nadine that touched Liz so deeply. Chance was devoted to his stepmother—and the feeling was visibly mutual.

Nadine studied Sara closely when Phillip introduced them. "So pretty," she commented approvingly. And then she frowned slightly. "But so very young."

"I'm really not as young as I look," Sara replied quickly, earnestly. "I'll be twenty-one in May."

"Twenty-one." Nadine sighed. "Little more than a girl."

"Mother . . ." Phillip murmured repressively.

Neal stepped forward to take Nadine's hand. "It seems we're going to be in-laws," he said. "Phillip's told us a great deal about you. You must be very proud of him."

Charmed, Nadine beamed. "Yes, I am. I'm so proud of *both* my boys," she added with a quick smile for Chance, who returned the smile lovingly, bringing a lump to Liz's throat. Nadine's smile faded as she looked back at Neal. "I understand Phillip will be working for you."

"Yes," Neal replied gently. "I expect him to be a great asset to my company."

"I have to tell you that I was hoping he'd move back to Birmingham after graduating. I miss him so much when he's away."

"I'm sure you do. But I know he and Sara will want to come to see you as often as they can."

"That would be nice," Nadine said wistfully.

Liz looked away from Phillip's mother only to find herself looking straight into Chance's eyes. He stood several feet away from her; his unwavering stare was as evocative as a touch, causing a decidedly physical response. Did he want to be alone with her as badly as she wanted to be with him? And would they have an opportunity during the next few days?

"I have to make a quick trip to a construction site for a few minutes," he announced rather apologetically, looking down at his watch. "We're shutting down for the remainder of the week because of the holiday and I have to see that everything's squared away."

"That's fine, dear. The rest of us will get to know each other better," Nadine assured him, smiling at Sara.

Chance glanced at Liz. "Ever been to Birmingham before?"

"No, I haven't," she replied.

"How about an abbreviated tour? You can ride along with me now, if you aren't too tired from your trip. My business will only take a few minutes, and Martha should have dinner ready by the time we get back."

Sara appeared intrigued, Phillip speculative, Neal concerned, and Nadine surprised and pleased that Chance was showing interest in Liz. Flushing lightly at being the focus of attention because of his casual invitation, Liz managed a smile. "Sounds interesting. I'd love to see more of Birmingham."

She lied, of course. She didn't care what city she was in, now that she was with Chance again.

In silence he escorted her out to his truck. He opened the passenger door for her, then steadied her as she climbed into the cab. Distracted by the feel of his hand on her arm, even through her lightweight coat, she nearly stumbled.

It took her three attempts to get her seat belt fastened. Finally she accomplished the feat just as Chance opened the driver's door and slid beneath the steering wheel. A burst of country-and-western music accompanied the roar of the engine when he turned the key in the ignition. He grimaced and reached out to turn the radio off.

"So, how have you been?" he asked as he guided the pickup out of the driveway.

"Fine," she lied. "And you?"

His reply was more honest: "Lousy."

"You've been sick?" she asked in quick concern.

He looked at her. "No." And then he focused on the road.

"Oh." She didn't know what else to say. Not until he let her know more of what was going on behind that impossible-to-read face of his.

Muttering incoherently, Chance looked quickly in his rearview mirror and whipped the truck into a deserted alley, where he shifted into park and killed the engine.

"What are you doing?" Liz demanded.

He faced her, laying one arm across the back of the seat so that his hand dangled only an inch or so from her shoulder—close enough for her to almost feel the heat from his skin. His eyes searched her face, so long and so intently that she squirmed uncomfortably.

"What is it?" she asked.

"You're so damned beautiful," he said. He touched the tips of his fingers to her hair. "I can't forget you, Liz."

"Were you *trying* to forget me?" she asked in little more than a whisper, all the sound she could get out past the lump in her throat.

"Yes."

His blunt answer made her flinch. "Why?"

His gaze met hers. It took him a moment to form his answer. "I didn't want you to break my heart."

She stared at him. "Did you—" She had to stop to clear her throat. "Did you really think that was a possibility?"

"Oh, yes." He sounded absolutely certain. "You're the only woman in the world who could."

She was stunned. "Chance—"

"We said some pretty harsh things to each other before I left," he said, his voice gruff. "I'm sorry. I didn't want to leave you that way."

"Neither did I," Liz answered unsteadily. "And I'm sorry for the things I said about you, Chance. You proved me wrong when you handled your talk with Phillip so well. Thank you for not doing anything to hurt Sara."

He took a deep breath. "Liz, I— Oh, hell." He leaned over and kissed her before either of them could think of anything else to say.

Liz had tried hard not to think about how much she'd missed Chance's kisses. She wouldn't have gotten through the past month without him if she'd allowed herself to dwell for too long on what they'd had. But now that she was with him again and his arms were around her, his mouth on hers, she knew her feelings for him hadn't changed, hadn't diminished. Rather she wanted him even more than she had before. His reluctant acceptance of Phillip's plans, his tenderness with his stepmother, the look in his eyes when he'd met Liz at the airport—each glimpse of his true nature made her love him more.

She wrapped her arms around his neck and strained to get closer to him, ignoring the restrictions of the narrow seat, not caring whether anyone should happen to see them. He murmured his approval, tightened his arms around her and deepened the kiss.

"Liz," he muttered when he broke away for air, "I've been going out of my mind with wanting you. It's been so long—" Breaking off, he kissed her again, sliding one hand down to stroke her stocking-covered thigh beneath the full skirt of her red dress.

Liz crowded closer to him, her fingers tangled in his crisp-soft hair, aching with hunger for him. His words had thrilled her, made her believe he'd been as miserable as she had since he'd left Atlanta. She dragged her mouth from beneath his with a gasp. "Oh, Chance, I've wanted you, too," she whispered, touching a hand to his hard, lean cheek. "So much."

"Why did you agree to come to Birmingham, Liz?" he asked urgently, his eyes searching her face. "Was it only for Sara's sake?"

"It wasn't for Sara's sake at all," she answered candidly, somewhat coyly. "It was for my own. I wanted— I needed to see you."

"Thank God." And he kissed her again.

She didn't know how long they sat in that dim, quiet alley, but all too soon they knew they had to leave. Kisses were no longer enough to satisfy either of them, and yet their families waited for them to return for dinner. Chance sighed deeply and pulled away from her with obvious reluctance. "I want to take you someplace where we can be completely alone," he grumbled, starting the engine. "I wouldn't let you out of bed for at least a week."

She smiled shakily, wistfully. "I think I'd like that."

"You only think you would?"

"I'm not sure a week would be long enough," she admitted.

He groaned and briefly closed his eyes. "You really know how to make me crazy, don't you?"

"I could say the same about you."

"We could forget about the family and go to your hotel room," he suggested only half-teasingly.

Sorely tempted, Liz shook her head. "I guess we'd better not."

Chance growled his frustration. "Then we may as well go to the construction site. If we sit here much longer, I'm going to get us arrested right here in this alley."

It would almost have been worth it, Liz thought longingly, resting her hand on Chance's rock-hard, denim-covered thigh.

# 11

THAT EVENING, ALL DURING dinner, Liz seethed with exasperation, wanting to kiss Chance and hit him, all at the same time.

It wasn't that he was rude to her family; far from it. He was unfailingly polite, but so distant that they might all have been total strangers just passing through his town.

Because she was slowly beginning to understand Chance, Liz thought she understood why he was so stiff with Neal and Sara—and even with Phillip, to a lesser extent. Chance was still hurting over Phillip's defection to Neal's company, and he grew strained when the conversation turned to business—just as he found it hard to be enthusiastic about wedding plans when that wedding served as a symbol of Phillip's defection and Chance's concern for Phillip's future.

And, Liz thought in frustration, Chance was still overly conscious of the contrast between his own modest, blue-collar roots and those of the old-money, established Archers of Atlanta.

Understanding the reasons for his behavior didn't make it any easier for her to excuse it.

Liz noticed the effect of Chance's reserved manner on her family. Neal became rather formal himself when he talked to Chance, though he warmed noticeably when his attention turned to Nadine. And Sara became increasingly nervous as the evening passed.

Liz swallowed a sigh and did her best to ease the tensions in the room by trying to keep the conversation light, innocuous. At one point she looked reprovingly at Chance, who'd seated himself beside her at the dinner table, but he either didn't understand her expression or—as she thought was more likely—chose to ignore it.

It wasn't long after dinner when Neal announced that he was rather tired from the busy day and was ready to head for his hotel room. Liz stood to accompany him, conscious of Chance's displeasure that she was leaving so early but deciding to overlook his frown.

Because Phillip really wanted her to do so, Sara was staying in the guest bedroom of the Cassidy home. Liz thought Sara looked a little lost when her aunt and father left, and her heart twisted in sympathy. Though she knew Sara would have to find her own way with her future in-laws, her first instinct was to protect her.

Buttoning her coat against the crisp December night air, Liz stepped out of the house toward the sedan Chance had rented for them. Neal had considerately gone out a few moments earlier to start the engine and heater so the car wouldn't be uncomfortably cold for Liz. She was halfway down the walk to the driveway when she heard Chance speak from behind her. "Liz, wait up a minute."

Her arms crossed defensively, she turned, head held high as he strode forcefully toward her. "What is it, Chance?"

"Why are you leaving now?" he demanded, taking advantage of their semiprivacy on the dimly lighted sidewalk. "Surely you knew I would have taken you to the hotel later. We could have had some time together."

"You think I can just ignore the way you behaved during dinner?" Liz asked incredulously. "Did you think I didn't notice the way you were treating my family?"

"I didn't do anything to slight your family. I was on my best behavior all evening, dammit," Chance said defensively.

"You were about as warm as an icicle and you know it!"

He sighed gustily, running a hand through his hair. "Look, I'm trying, okay? It's not easy."

She softened. "I know it isn't easy, Chance. I know you're still trying to come to terms with it all. But your stiffness upsets Sara. She assumes you disapprove of her."

"I'll try to ease up," he promised in a mutter.

"Thank you." She glanced behind her at the car where Neal waited patiently behind the wheel. "I have to go. I'll see you in the morning."

His gaze followed hers to the car and he hesitated. "The hell with it," he muttered reaching out to pull her into his arms. His kiss was brief, but hard enough and hot enough to make her melt. She quickly steadied herself when he pulled away.

"Good night, Liz."

"Good night, Chance," she whispered, then ran to the car. She was aware that Chance stood where he was, coatless in the chilly night air, until Neal had driven out of sight.

"You and Chance have put your quarrel behind you?" Neal asked after a few moments of deliberate silence.

"We're working on it," Liz murmured, thinking of Chance's promise to try harder with her family despite his misgivings about the entire situation.

"Why do you suppose the guy invited us here when it's clear he wishes we hadn't come?" Neal demanded. "He was about as welcoming as a Doberman pinscher."

"He's trying, Neal. Surely you understand how difficult it is for him to accept Phillip's sudden decision to go to work for you. They'd planned for so long for Phillip to join Chance after graduation. Chance had really looked forward to that day."

"So why invite us here for the holidays if he still resents us?"

"He did that for Phillip's sake, and for Nadine's. To give Phillip an opportunity to introduce his new family to his mother, and maybe to prove that this is really what he wants. He's not going to drive Phillip away, as our father did us, Neal. He's resolved to salvage their relationship, despite the hurt they've both suffered."

"Because of your warnings to him?"

"Maybe I had something to do with his decision," she said hesitantly.

Neal nodded. "Chance is in love with you, Liz."

"What makes you say that?"

"I watched him," Neal replied as though that was all the answer required. Liz shouldn't have been so surprised that he'd sensed the intensity of the emotions sizzling between her and Chance. But love? Was Chance *in love* with her?

Had that been what he'd meant when he'd said she could break his heart?

Lost in thought, Liz was silent during the short drive to the hotel. Neal let her be, understanding that she needed time to reflect.

THE HOTEL ROOM WAS quite luxurious. Plush carpeting, tasteful colors and accessories, a bed that might have been comfortable if Liz hadn't been so restless. Finally, sometime after midnight, she gave up trying to sleep and climbed out of bed to pace to the window, where she stared sightlessly out at the lights of Birmingham and thought of Chance.

She heard a soft knocking on the door.

Clutching her robe more closely around her, she crossed the room to stand with one hand on the security chain. "Who is it?" she asked quietly.

"It's Chance."

She opened the door. He stood with one hand on the doorjamb, wearing the same clothes he'd had on at dinner along with his leather jacket. "I take it you weren't asleep?" he asked.

"You knew I wouldn't be," she accused him, stepping aside to allow him to enter. "Come in out of the hallway."

He looked around pointedly as he walked in. "You and your brother don't have connecting rooms, I hope?"

"No. But he is next door."

Chance closed the door behind him, then deliberately slid the chain into place. "Then we'll have to be quiet, won't we?"

She moistened her lips. "I suppose we will."

He shrugged out of his jacket and tossed it aside. "Have you forgiven me yet?"

"About dinner, you mean?" she asked distractedly, watching as he reached for the top button of his shirt. She really should say something about his apparent assumption that he could just walk right into her room and start taking his clothes off, she thought. But, oh, how she wanted him out of those clothes!

His shirt fell over the same chair on which his jacket had landed. "Yes."

"Were you—" Her voice died when he unsnapped his jeans. Eyes glued in fascination to the movements of his strong, tanned hands, she cleared her throat and tried again. "Were you nicer to Sara after we left?"

"I tried. She claimed she was tired and turned in early." Jeans unzipped, he kicked off his boots. "Do you really want to talk about our families now?"

"No," she whispered, letting her robe part to reveal the thin silk gown she wore beneath it.

She hadn't fully realized quite how much she'd missed his sexy smile until now. Tossing his jeans in the general vicinity of his other clothes, he sauntered purposefully toward her, unself-consciously nude, boldly aroused. "Neither do I," he murmured and slid the robe from her shoulders.

She opened her mouth to his kiss, her head falling back to allow him better access. By the time the kiss ended, they were both naked.

The bed was so much more comfortable when Chance shared it with her. Liz hadn't noticed before how smooth and fragrant the sheets were, nor how deliciously soft the mattress and pillows. She noticed now, as she and Chance sank into them, their bodies locked in a sensual embrace. He lay beneath her, his hands on her hips, guiding her onto him. She arched to fill herself with him, and felt as though she'd come home after a long, lonely journey.

"Oh, God, Liz, I've missed you. Ached for you," Chance muttered, holding her tightly to him, delaying the race toward culmination as long as he could.

She knew his words were as close as he'd ever come to a flowery declaration. His difficulty in expressing his feelings made the words all the more precious to her. "I've missed you, too, Chance," she whispered, aching with the pleasure-pain of being joined with him, so close to fulfillment. "Nothing's been the same for me since you left Atlanta."

"For me, neither," he admitted. "Liz, I—" He broke off with a groan, his fingers digging into her hips, his body surging into the rhythm of lovemaking. "I can't wait any longer," he muttered, his jaw clenched with the effort of his restraint.

"Neither can I," she gasped, tightening around him. "Oh, Chance."

After that, words were no longer necessary.

JUST BEFORE DAWN Chance slipped out of the room. Neither of them had slept more than a few moments, but Liz didn't complain. Smiling dreamily, she snuggled into the pillows after he left and noted in pleasure that the pillowcases still bore the scent of his aftershave.

He still hadn't told her he loved her, but she hoped that he did. Could he have made love to her so tenderly, so totally, if he didn't love her at least a little?

She fell into a deep, dreamless sleep, not awakening until the telephone rang three hours later. Neal was calling to see if she was going to join him downstairs for breakfast. Hurriedly, she showered and dressed.

She couldn't quite meet her brother's gaze as they sat down to breakfast on opposite sides of a cozy table for two in a quiet corner of the hotel restaurant. She hid behind a menu. "I'm rather hungry this morning," she said airily. "What are you having?"

"The Belgian waffles."

"That sounds good. With juice and coffee," she added to the hovering waitress, who scurried away with their orders—and the menu, unfortunately.

"Doesn't seem like Christmas Eve, does it?" she asked, "This is the first time since my divorce that I've spent Christmas away from Atlanta."

"Liz."

She cleared her throat and studied her fingernails. "Yes, Neal?"

"Did you sleep well?"

"Yes, thank you," she replied, telling herself she wasn't really lying. She'd slept very well during those three short hours after Chance left. She picked up her water glass, more to have something to do with her hands than because she was really thirsty. "And you?"

"I'm never really comfortable when I'm not in my own bed," Neal answered. "Chance doesn't have the same problem, I guess."

Liz choked on a gulp of water. Coughing frantically into a napkin, she glared at her wryly amused brother. "What was that supposed to mean?" she demanded when she could speak.

"I heard the knock on your door. I didn't think it was maid service after midnight."

Did nothing *ever* escape him? Liz wondered in exasperation. "So you assumed it was Chance?"

He shrugged. "I didn't hold a water glass to the wall to identify voices, but, yes, I assumed it was Chance."

She sighed. "You're right. It was."

"You're a grown woman, Liz. I'm not asking for excuses or explanations."

"Nor will you receive them," she answered spiritedly. "So why did you bother to bring this up?"

He gave her the smile that had always made her long to hit him when she was a teenager. It had much the same effect now. "I just wanted you to know I knew," he said, then looked up in apparent pleasure when the waitress reappeared with their breakfasts. "Looks good. I'm really hungry this morning."

*Brothers*, Liz thought with a frown, reaching gratefully for her coffee. Darned if she wouldn't *help* Sara fix him up with Devon when they got back to Atlanta, she decided abruptly. Though poor Devon hadn't done anything to annoy her, it would serve Neal right to find himself entangled in Sara's matchmaking scheme!

THE CASSIDYS' housekeeper, Martha, opened the door when Liz rang the bell a couple of hours later, at the time they'd arranged the night before. She led them into the den, where Nadine sat in her wheelchair beside the blazing fireplace, facing the colorfully decorated Christmas tree as she read a novel. She laid the book on her lap and greeted Liz and Neal with a warm smile. "Good morning. Did you rest well?"

"Very well, thank you," Liz answered with a quick, don't-you-dare-dispute-me look at her brother.

Neal smiled blandly in response. "Where's Sara?" he asked.

"Phillip is showing her around Birmingham—some of the places he hangs out when he's home," Nadine disclosed. "Chance is in his room going over some paperwork for his business, Liz. Why don't you tell him you're here? He'll work all day if we let him."

"Oh, I—"

Ignoring Liz's automatic protest, Nadine waved a slender hand toward the hallway. "It's the last door on the left. He has the master suite."

Ignoring Neal's smug smile, Liz resignedly obeyed Nadine's gentle command.

The last door on the left was closed. Liz moistened her lips and knocked twice.

"Okay, Martha, I'm—" He stopped talking when he saw her, then smiled. "Good morning."

Her knees suddenly feeling weak, she clung to the doorway for support. She returned his smile, feeling like a giddy, infatuated schoolgirl—and she liked the feeling! "Good morning."

He tugged her inside the room and kissed her thoroughly, lingeringly. "You're beautiful this morning," he murmured when he released her. "I like that sweater."

She touched the neckline of the white cashmere garment self-consciously. She'd worn it, along with her gray wool slacks, because she knew the outfit looked good on her, and she'd wanted to please Chance. "Thank you."

She looked away from the heat in his eyes, needing a moment to regain her composure. "So this is the master's room," she said lightly, studying the masculine decor. The walls were knotty pine, the furniture American Colonial, the colors rich greens and deep burgundy. Landscapes hung on the wall—a sunrise over water, a meandering dirt road leading past an old house into autumn woods. They appeared to have been painted by the same artist. "Someone you know?" she asked, studying the muted colors of the sunrise.

"My mother," he answered. "She was good, wasn't she?"

"Yes, she was," Liz agreed sincerely, turning to face him again. "Did she ever show her work?"

He shook his head. "Her painting was a hobby. She took it up after I was born."

"How did she die?" Liz asked gently, realizing he'd never said.

"A cerebral hemorrhage. One minute she was watching TV with my dad, the next she was gone. She probably never even knew what was happening."

She didn't offer her sympathy—not with words, though she knew he read her feelings in her eyes. "Do you remember her?"

He nodded. "Yes. Quite well, considering how young I was when she died."

"I'm glad you have those memories."

He looked pleased by her words. "So am I."

"Was it difficult for you to accept Nadine as your stepmother?" Liz asked, wondering if he'd been as resistant to his father's marriage as he was to his brother's.

Chance hesitated, then shrugged. "I wasn't exactly pleased when my father started dating her. It took her all of about a week to win me over. She's a very special woman. She made my father happy—and she gave me a brother."

Touched by his words, Liz asked gravely, "How serious is her condition?"

"We don't know how much longer we have together," Chance replied quietly. "We've agreed to enjoy the time we have without worrying about the future."

"That's a very wise decision."

"We thought so." Chance hesitated, then said gruffly, "Nadine will have a home with me as long as it's possible for me to provide care for her. I know Phillip would take her if he could, but he's young and just starting out. He couldn't take care of her as well as I do, and we all know that. So she'll stay with me."

Was he telling her this to test her feelings about his obligation to his stepmother? Liz wondered, even as she replied, "Of course, she will. Knowing you, I would never expect anything else. She's very lucky to have you, Chance."

Because she wasn't quite ready for him to read her feelings for him in her eyes—as he surely would if she continued to look at him—she turned her attention back to the furnishings of his room. A small desk sat in one corner, its surface covered with papers, a calculator, pencils, what looked like rolled-up blueprints. "Do you work here often?"

"Sometimes, at night. I have an office, of course, but I bring work home as often as not."

"I can identify with that," she said with a quick laugh.

"You really like your business, don't you, Liz?"

She was surprised that he asked. "Of course. I love my work."

"And are you as committed to Atlanta? Or have you ever considered living anywhere else?"

Her chest tightened at the implications of the seemingly innocent question. "I love Atlanta, of course, but I'm not permanently rooted there. As for my business— Well, people get married everywhere, don't they?"

"Yeah. I guess they do."

The silence that followed seemed fraught with questions too important to be asked casually. Liz cleared her throat and, noticing a carved wooden box on his dresser, picked it up. It just fit into the palm of her hand. "This is lovely. It looks very old. Is it?"

"It was my great-grandmother's." Chance's voice deepened. Liz wondered what was so important about the box to make him sound so serious. "Look inside," he urged, taking a step closer to stand behind her—not touching, but near enough that she could almost feel his breath against the back of her neck.

Her hands weren't quite steady when she lifted the hinged lid.

The ring inside was beautiful. A square-cut diamond had been set in rose gold, with two baguettes glinting at either side. "How lovely," she breathed, realizing that the ring was every bit as old as the box. "Was it your great-grandmother's?"

"Yes. My great-grandfather was a milkman," Chance explained. "He delivered milk from the back of a horse-drawn wagon. He didn't make a great deal of money, but he wanted his bride to have a very special ring. He took two other jobs to earn enough to have this made for her. My great-grandmother told her son that she hardly saw him during their two-year engagement, because he was working so many hours. He gave her this ring on their wedding day."

"What a wonderful story. He must have loved her very much."

"Yes. They were married for fifty years. When their son, my grandfather, brought a bride home from a trip east, his mother gave him the ring for his wife, telling him she wanted it to be passed from generation to generation as a sign of the love she and her husband had shared, on which they'd founded their family. So, when my father married my mother, this was the ring she wore. It's been kept in this box since she died. Nadine chose not to wear it. She seemed to think only one bride from each generation should have the honor."

"Shouldn't you keep it in a safe?" Liz asked in concern, surprised that Chance would keep such a precious heirloom sitting out in the open. "What if it was stolen?"

"I get more pleasure having it where I can look at it sometimes than I would having it locked in a safe," Chance answered simply.

The response was typically Chance. Liz thought he'd probably never believe anyone would dare steal his family ring from him.

Chance cleared his throat. "I offered the ring to Phillip for Sara when he and I talked that night in Atlanta."

Liz looked at him in unconcealed surprise. "You did?"

He nodded. "He turned it down." The faintest hint of relief was evident in his voice. "He said he'd always thought the ring should go to my wife, because I'm the eldest and because I was named after our great-grandfather."

Liz's trembling intensified, though she tried hard to hide it from Chance's too-sharp eyes. "That was very unselfish of him," she whispered.

Chance nodded. "Yeah. I thought so."

She told herself to close the box and change the subject, but couldn't. "Have you looked for someone to wear this ring, Chance?"

"Yes," he answered honestly. "I've looked, and waited, and hoped. But I could never find anyone who met the image I'd created of the perfect wife."

"What was she like—the woman you were looking for?" she asked, even more daringly.

He shrugged. "Young. Pretty. A little sheltered, a little shy. Someone who'd want me to take care of her, who wouldn't care whether I had a degree or a fancy, society life-style. Someone who'd be content to stay home and take care of our kids and Nadine while I worked to support us."

A sharp pain ripped through her. Liz slowly closed the box, looking down at its carved lid as she thought of how very different she was from the woman of Chance's fantasy. Not that she cared about his lack of formal education or his quiet life-style, of course, but the rest of it— Well, she wasn't so young, definitely not sheltered, not at all shy. And though she'd love to have children, she couldn't imagine ever being content to stay home while her husband worked to support her.

Liz thrived on her work, loved being productive and successful at what she did.

"That's the type of woman I used to think I wanted for my wife," Chance continued steadily. Liz could almost feel him watching her, though she didn't look up. "I've recently changed my mind about some of those requirements."

She couldn't find her voice to ask him to elaborate, but he did, anyway. "Now," he said carefully, deliberately, "I find myself wanting a completely different type of woman. One who has experienced life and knows what she wants from it. One who is comfortable in the business world that sometimes confuses the hell out of me. One who doesn't hesitate to speak her mind to me. One who sees my faults and my shortcomings and then looks past them. One who wants me as much as I want her."

Liz closed her eyes, overwhelmed by his words. They were so devastating coming from Chance, who often struggled to express his feelings clearly.

"I don't know if I've got enough to offer a woman like that," Chance said quietly. "Maybe she wouldn't be interested in a man who brought himself up the hard way from a 'working-class' background. A man who doesn't know opera from Oprah, who couldn't care less about trends and fashions, who sometimes spends too much time on construction sites and not enough at social events."

"A man," he added more forcefully, "who is sometimes bossy and arrogant, but truly believes the right woman could help him change."

"The right woman wouldn't want you to change," Liz whispered, tears brimming in her eyes. "If the woman you described is really so bright, she'd appreciate your honesty, your strength, your loyal, sometimes misguided sense of responsibility to your family, your willingness to admit that you aren't perfect." Her ex-husband had never confessed his faults, never offered to change. He would never have made himself that vulnerable—to her or anyone else.

Chance placed his hands on her shoulders, and Liz's tears fell faster when she felt the tremors in those strong, capable hands. "I love you, Liz."

Her breath caught in a sob. "I love you, too."

He released a long, ragged breath. He rested his cheek on her hair. "I know we haven't known each other very long, but I've been miserable without you this past month. I want you with me all the time. Will you marry me? Wear my great-grandmother's ring?"

She turned in his arms, making no effort to hide the trail of tears on her cheeks. It wasn't necessary for her to take time to consider his utterly unexpected proposal. "I would be honored," she said.

He groaned and covered her mouth with his own. "I love you," he murmured when he finally raised his head. "More than I ever thought I'd love anyone."

"Oh, Chance."

A door slammed somewhere in the house, followed by a roar that sounded like Phillip's agitated voice. Reluctantly, Chance lifted his head and looked toward the doorway. "What in the—?"

A muted babble of voices carried down the hallway. Something was very wrong in the den.

Chance snatched the ring out of the wooden box, shoving it without ceremony onto Liz's left hand. "Sorry," he muttered, apologizing for the lack of romance in the gesture. "Something tells me I'm going to need to see you wearing this."

It seemed a good omen that the ring fit almost perfectly. Curling her fingers protectively around it, she allowed Chance to tow her down the hallway toward the den, her head still spinning at the momentous decision she had just made.

She was going to marry Chance Cassidy—a man she'd known only a month, and with whom she'd spent less than a week together. Yet nothing in her life had ever felt more right.

# 12

LOOKING SMALL and defenseless, Sara sat in an over-size armchair, sobbing as though her heart were break-ing. Neal stood beside her, his expression harried as he patted her shoulder and tried to get her to talk to him. Phillip paced the room like a wild man, his arms flail-ing, loudly proclaiming that he simply didn't under-stand women. From her wheelchair, Nadine stared at the others in openmouthed bewilderment, distressed by Sara's crying and Phillip's ranting.

"What the *hell* is going on in here?" Chance de-manded, surveying the scene in astonishment.

"She's called off the wedding!" Phillip answered fu-riously, swinging an arm toward Sara. "Broken our engagement! Can you believe that? *Women!*"

Liz couldn't have been more shocked if the roof had caved in. "Sara?" she asked, hurrying to her distraught niece. "Is this true?"

"Yes," Sara wailed. "I have. I'm so so-o-r-r-y."

"You don't want to marry Phillip?" Liz demanded, staring hard at her niece's wretched expression.

Sara tried to answer, but dissolved into renewed weeping.

"Of *course*, she wants to marry me," Phillip all but shouted. "For God's sake, Sara, tell us what's wrong."

"Everything's wrong! I can't marry you, Phillip. I'm sorry, but it's over."

Again, it was Chance who spoke most clearly in the uproar that followed. "Phillip, be quiet a minute," he ordered sharply. "Let's try to get to the bottom of this."

He crossed the room to where Sara sat, kneeling in front of her with one hand resting on an arm of the chair. "Sara, does this have anything to do with me?"

Sara started and looked quickly up at her father, as if asking for intervention. Neal shook his head. "Answer him, Sara," he said gently.

Visibly intimidated, Sara darted a quick, wet glance at Chance, then nodded forlornly.

"*What—?*" Phillip started forward, only to stop short when Chance motioned for him to stay put.

"Tell me why, Sara," Chance urged, his voice low, even.

Sara drew a deep, catching breath. "You and Phillip were so close before he met me," she said. "He loves you so much. And now I've come between you. You were hurt and he feels guilty for hurting you, and...and you think I'm too young and immature to marry him and...and you probably think I'm not good enough for him because my parents were never married," she added all in one shaky rush.

"Sara!" Neal looked stricken.

Liz was stunned. She'd never realized how deeply Sara had been affected by her mother's selfish abandonment. She'd always thought—always hoped—that the love and devotion Neal had given his daughter had more than compensated for Lynn's disinterest. "Oh, Sara," she whispered.

Even Phillip seemed floored. "Sara. Darling," he said unsteadily. "Surely you don't think—"

Still kneeling in front of her, Chance took Sara's hands firmly in his own, his expression unchanged by the revelation. "I didn't even know about that," he said quietly. "And now that I do, it doesn't make the least bit of difference."

"But you came to Atlanta to stop the wedding," Sara whispered miserably.

"Yes," Chance admitted. "I did. I thought Phillip was making a mistake. But we've talked it through and Phillip apologized for sending a letter instead of having it out with me, face-to-face. I won't pretend that I'm not disappointed about his decision to stay in Atlanta rather than coming home to work with me—I am. But he has the right to make his own decisions about his future. I realize that now."

Sara still looked doubtful. "But you've been so cool to him. He said he thought you were mad at him—and I knew it was all my fault."

"I'm not angry," Chance assured her firmly. "If I've been distant, it's because I didn't really know how to act. I'm not very good in social situations, Sara. I don't always know what to say to people I don't know very well—or even to the ones who mean the most to me, sometimes," he admitted with a glance at Liz. "I'd like you to reconsider your decision to end your engagement. If Phillip is lucky enough to marry you, I want you to be assured that it will be with the full support and approval of his family."

Sara sniffed. "You don't still think we're too young?"

Chance hesitated, then shrugged. "I guess only the two of you can know about that. You're both adults, and if you think you're ready to be married, then who am I to say differently?"

"I love Phillip so much," Sara whispered tearfully. "I know he and I haven't known each other for a long time, but that doesn't matter for us. We knew from the beginning that we were right for each other."

"Yeah, well—" Chance cleared his throat, suddenly looking rather endearingly sheepish in Liz's admittedly biased eyes. "Maybe I wouldn't have understood that a month ago. But since I fell in love in less than five days while I was in Atlanta, I guess I know exactly what you mean."

Sara's tears stopped. She cocked her head, immediately intrigued. "You fell in love with someone in Atlanta?" she asked. "Who—?"

And then she caught her breath and looked up at Liz. "Aunt Liz! You?"

Liz smiled unsteadily and nodded.

Chance rose and reached for Liz's hand. "We're getting married."

"Married?" Sara, Phillip, Nadine and Neal echoed in almost perfect unison.

Chance winced. "I can tell I've made myself real popular lately."

Phillip stepped forward first, his hand outstretched to his brother. "Congratulations, Chance. I couldn't have picked a better match for you if I'd tried."

Chance thanked his brother, then turned to receive his stepmother's tender hug, assuring her quietly that she and Liz would get along beautifully when they all lived together as a family.

Swiping hastily at her tear-streaked cheeks, Sara rose to put her arms around her aunt. "I'm happy for you, Aunt Liz," she said, then asked in a whisper, "You really love him?"

Liz chuckled and hugged Sara tightly. "Yes, I do," she murmured, giving her lover a teasing glance. "And you will, too, when you get to know him better," she murmured into Sara's ear.

Neal rested a hand on Liz's shoulder. "You're sure?" he asked quietly.

Her heart twisting at the deep lines carved around his mouth from Sara's emotional outburst, Liz reached up to kiss his cheek. "I'm very sure, Neal."

"I guess you're old enough to know what you're doing," he commented with a smile.

"Yes." She placed her hand in Chance's again, reading the love in his eyes. "I know exactly what I'm doing."

A WOODEN DECK RAN the length of Chance's house at the back, overlooking a spacious, beautifully landscaped lawn. Liz found Neal there later that afternoon when she slipped away from the den where Chance, Phillip and Sara were watching a Christmas Eve football game while Nadine rested from the events of the morning.

"Neal?" Liz asked, stepping through the sliding-glass doors and shivering in the cool December air. "Shouldn't you be wearing your jacket if you're going to stand outside?"

He gave her a crooked smile. "Playing the mother hen, Liz?"

"Someone has to watch out for you," she retorted, slipping her hand beneath his arm. "What're you doing out here?"

"Just needed a few minutes alone," Neal answered lightly. "You know how I get when there are too many people around."

"Want me to go back in?"

He shook his head. "You don't count."

"I'm not sure if that was a compliment or an insult."

Neal chuckled. "I'll let you think about it."

Liz leaned comfortably against his arm, her cheek against his shoulder. They stood that way in familiar silence for a few long moments. When she spoke, Liz chose her words carefully. "You can't let Sara's words bother you too much, Neal. She was nervous and upset. Engagements are a stressful time, with so much to do and so many decisions ahead. And Sara's so accustomed to having everyone accept her unconditionally that it bothered her badly to think that Chance didn't approve of her for Phillip."

"So she automatically assumed it was because she was born illegitimately," Neal said bleakly. "Dammit, Liz. That never would have occurred to her now if it hadn't bothered her over the years. I never wanted her to feel she had to apologize for the circumstances of her birth. I tried so hard to make it up to her—but I guess it wasn't enough."

"Of course, it was enough, Neal," Liz replied firmly, knowing her brother's overdeveloped sense of responsibility and duty would haunt him if he thought he'd failed Sara in any way. Again she saw how very much alike Neal and Chance were in some ways. And maybe that was one of the reasons she loved him.

"You're a wonderful father to Sara. She adores you. She was simply trying to understand Chance's reservations about the engagement and she grabbed at the first possibility that occurred to her. You can't blame yourself because Lynn was so self-centered."

"Chance really didn't know? You didn't tell him?"

"Of course not. He did some research about you, of course, just as you would have done if the circumstances had been reversed," she added, in case Neal should object. "That was one thing he couldn't find out, although he learned that Sara's mother disappeared a long time ago. I didn't discuss it with him, because I didn't think your past was any of his concern before."

"You may as well tell him the whole story, now that he's going to be so close to the family."

"I will. The *real* story," Liz added. "How you tried to talk Lynn into marrying you for your child's sake, how she used your vulnerability with the baby to bleed you for money and then left you with Sara and little else. How you worked so hard to raise Sara in a loving home and to provide the best you could for her, building a successful business empire from nothing more than a small inheritance from Grandfather Davison."

"Saint Neal," he said, mocking her loyal defense.

She smiled. "Not quite. But close."

Neal looked around the yard and behind them at the house. "Think you'll be happy here?"

"Yes," she replied without any hesitation.

"He's an interesting guy. He handled that scene with Sara very nicely."

"He did, didn't he?"

"You know," Neal added thoughtfully, "he reminds me of someone, but I can't decide who it is."

Liz laughed, deciding not to enlighten him at the moment. He probably wouldn't believe her, anyway.

PLEASANTLY SATED and drowsy, Liz snuggled against Chance's bare shoulder, her hand curled over his heart. "I love you," she whispered into the silent darkness of the hotel room. It was after midnight—which made it Christmas. She couldn't remember ever being happier.

"So when are you going to marry me?" Chance asked in an equally contented murmur.

"We haven't talked about that, have we?"

"No. I'd like it to be soon."

"I hope early summer is soon enough."

"Summer?" Chance repeated, jostling her when he rose up on one elbow to stare down at her. "Summer is at least six months away."

"Chance, I have weddings scheduled through June, including Sara's. I can't just walk away from my commitments to those clients. I'll have to decide what to do with the business, make arrangements to start a similar business here, research the Birmingham area for available services and suppliers, make plans for the move . . ."

He sighed gustily. "All right, I get the picture. You can't just drop everything and walk away."

"No."

He fell back on the bed, disgruntled but resigned. "All right. You have until the middle of July. But I intend to see you every chance I get during that time. And I don't even want to think about the phone bills."

"I hope that's enough time to take care of everything," Liz fretted.

"Make it enough time," he ordered, his patience at an end.

She decided she'd work more on his natural bossiness later. For now, there were other things she'd rather do with him. She rolled smoothly on top of him and covered his mouth with her own, effectively putting an end to the conversation.

CHRISTMAS DAY in the Cassidy household was a warm, festive event, Liz thought as she wandered through the house. Enticing aromas of cinnamon, nutmeg and roast turkey drifted from the kitchen, carols played softly from artfully concealed speakers in the den, multicolored tree lights twinkled cheerfully above piles of gaily wrapped packages. Earlier Phillip had volunteered to hand out the gifts, with Sara as his enthusiastic assistant.

The others seemed rather confused by the gifts Liz and Chance exchanged. A subscription to the *Wall Street Journal* for Chance, an expensive leather softball glove for Liz. Liz was happy that Chance seemed pleased with his present. She hadn't wanted him to think her foolish or condescending, but she'd wanted him to know that she thought he was as clever a businessman as Neal or Phillip—if not more so.

Sara seemed the most perplexed when the softball glove moved Liz almost to tears. "I suppose there's a story behind this?" she asked dryly.

Liz nodded, looking toward Chance, who'd remembered her confession that she'd always wanted to play softball, but hadn't been allowed by her overly strict parents.

"Maybe we can have a game of catch in the backyard after lunch?" Chance asked Liz, smiling tenderly at her expression.

The Cassidy diamond rested comfortably on the hand she held out to him, as though it had been meant for her. "I'd like that," she told him, basking in the warmth of his smile. "I'd like that a lot."

Not caring that they were the focus of attention, Chance kissed her lingeringly. "Merry Christmas, Liz," he murmured.

"Merry Christmas, Chance," she whispered in return, knowing his love was the most precious gift she would ever receive.

**HARLEQUIN** *Temptation*

**Rebels & Rogues**

**Jackson:** Honesty was his policy...
and the price he demanded of the woman
he loved.

**THE LAST HONEST MAN**
by Leandra Logan
Temptation #393, May 1992

All men are not created equal. Some are
rough around the edges. Tough-minded but
tenderhearted. Incredibly sexy. The tempting
fulfillment of every woman's fantasy.

When it's time to fight for what they believe in,
to win that special woman, our Rebels and Rogues
are heroes at heart. Twelve Rebels and Rogues,
one each month in 1992, only from
Harlequin Temptation!

# HARLEQUIN PROUDLY PRESENTS A
# DAZZLING CONCEPT IN ROMANCE FICTION

### One small town,
### twelve terrific love stories.

## TYLER—GREAT READING... GREAT SAVINGS...
## AND A FABULOUS FREE GIFT

Each book set in Tyler is a self-contained love story;
together, the twelve novels stitch the fabric of
the community.

By collecting proofs-of-purchase found in each Tyler
book, you can receive a fabulous gift, ABSOLUTELY
FREE! And use our special Tyler coupons to save on
your next Tyler book purchase.

Join us for the third Tyler book, WISCONSIN
WEDDING by Carla Neggers, available in May.

---

Following the success of WITH THIS RING,
Harlequin cordially invites you to enjoy the
romance of the wedding season with

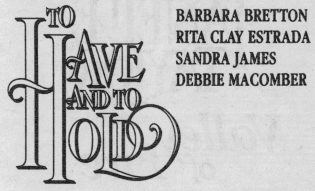

**BARBARA BRETTON
RITA CLAY ESTRADA
SANDRA JAMES
DEBBIE MACOMBER**

A collection of romantic stories that celebrate the joy,
excitement, and mishaps of planning that special day
by these four award-winning Harlequin authors.

**Available in April at your favorite Harlequin
retail outlets.**

## "GET AWAY FROM IT ALL" SWEEPSTAKES

# HERE'S HOW THE SWEEPSTAKES WORKS

### NO PURCHASE NECESSARY

To enter each drawing, complete the appropriate Official Entry Form or a 3" by 5" index card by hand-printing your name, address and phone number and the trip destination that the entry is being submitted for (i.e., Caneel Bay, Canyon Ranch or London and the English Countryside) and mailing it to: Get Away From It All Sweepstakes, P.O. Box 1397, Buffalo, New York 14269-1397.

No responsibility is assumed for lost, late or misdirected mail. Entries must be sent separately with first class postage affixed, and be received by: 4/15/92 for the Caneel Bay Vacation Drawing, 5/15/92 for the Canyon Ranch Vacation Drawing and 6/15/92 for the London and the English Countryside Vacation Drawing. Sweepstakes is open to residents of the U.S. (except Puerto Rico) and Canada, 21 years of age or older as of 5/31/92.

For complete rules send a self-addressed, stamped (WA residents need not affix return postage) envelope to: Get Away From It All Sweepstakes, P.O. Box 4892, Blair, NE 68009.

© 1992 HARLEQUIN ENTERPRISES LTD.                    SWP-RLS

---

## "GET AWAY FROM IT ALL" SWEEPSTAKES

# HERE'S HOW THE SWEEPSTAKES WORKS

### NO PURCHASE NECESSARY

To enter each drawing, complete the appropriate Official Entry Form or a 3" by 5" index card by hand-printing your name, address and phone number and the trip destination that the entry is being submitted for (i.e., Caneel Bay, Canyon Ranch or London and the English Countryside) and mailing it to: Get Away From It All Sweepstakes, P.O. Box 1397, Buffalo, New York 14269-1397.

No responsibility is assumed for lost, late or misdirected mail. Entries must be sent separately with first class postage affixed, and be received by: 4/15/92 for the Caneel Bay Vacation Drawing, 5/15/92 for the Canyon Ranch Vacation Drawing and 6/15/92 for the London and the English Countryside Vacation Drawing. Sweepstakes is open to residents of the U.S. (except Puerto Rico) and Canada, 21 years of age or older as of 5/31/92.

For complete rules send a self-addressed, stamped (WA residents need not affix return postage) envelope to: Get Away From It All Sweepstakes, P.O. Box 4892, Blair, NE 68009.

© 1992 HARLEQUIN ENTERPRISES LTD.                    SWP-RLS

## "GET AWAY FROM IT ALL"

### Brand-new Subscribers-Only Sweepstakes

# OFFICIAL ENTRY FORM

This entry must be received by: May 15, 1992
This month's winner will be notified by: May 31, 1992
Trip must be taken between: June 30, 1992—June 30, 1993

**YES,** I want to win the Canyon Ranch vacation for two. I understand the prize includes round-trip airfare and the two additional prizes revealed in the BONUS PRIZES insert.

Name _____

Address _____

City _____

State/Prov._____ Zip/Postal Code_____

Daytime phone number _____
(Area Code)

Return entries with invoice in envelope provided. Each book in this shipment has two entry coupons — and the more coupons you enter, the better your chances of winning!
© 1992 HARLEQUIN ENTERPRISES LTD. 2M-CPN

---

## "GET AWAY FROM IT ALL"

### Brand-new Subscribers-Only Sweepstakes

# OFFICIAL ENTRY FORM

This entry must be received by: May 15, 1992
This month's winner will be notified by: May 31, 1992
Trip must be taken between: June 30, 1992—June 30, 1993

**YES,** I want to win the Canyon Ranch vacation for two. I understand the prize includes round-trip airfare and the two additional prizes revealed in the BONUS PRIZES insert.

Name _____

Address _____

City _____

State/Prov._____ Zip/Postal Code_____

Daytime phone number _____
(Area Code)

Return entries with invoice in envelope provided. Each book in this shipment has two entry coupons — and the more coupons you enter, the better your chances of winning!
© 1992 HARLEQUIN ENTERPRISES LTD. 2M-CPN